YEARS OF
ORIGINAL
WRITING

Celebrating ten years of risk-taking writing for risk-taking readers.

JM Originals was launched in 2015 to champion distinctive, experimental, genre-defying fiction and non-fiction. From memoirs and short stories to literary and speculative fiction, it is a place where readers can find something, well, *original*.

JM Originals is unlike any other list out there, with its editors having sole say in the books that get published on the list. The buck stops with them and that is what makes things so exciting: they can publish from the heart, or on a hunch, or because they just really, really like the words they've read. As well as championing new writing, we're also excited by new design: every JM Original is published with a bespoke cover by an up-and-coming illustrator from Liverpool John Moores University.

In the past ten years, many of our Originals authors have won or been shortlisted for a whole host of prizes including the Booker Prize, the Desmond Elliott Prize, the Women's Prize for Fiction, the Portico Prize and the Edge Hill Short Story Prize. Our hope for our wonderful authors is that JM Originals will be the first step in their publishing journey and that they will continue writing books for John Murray well into the future.

JM Originals

X @j_m_originals ◎ @johnmurrays
johnmurraypress.co.uk

T0271606

Portraits at the Palace of Creativity and Wrecking

Han Smith

JM ORIGINALS

First published in Great Britain in 2024 by JM Originals
An Imprint of John Murray (Publishers)

4

Trade Paperback ISBN 9781399814256
ebook ISBN 9781399814263

Typeset in Minion Pro by Manipal Technologies Limited

Printed and bound in Great Britain by Clays Ltd, Elcograf S.p.A.

John Murray policy is to use papers that are natural, renewable and recyclable
products and made from wood grown in sustainable forests. The logging and
manufacturing processes are expected to conform to the environmental
regulations of the country of origin.

John Murray (Publishers)
Carmelite House
50 Victoria Embankment
London EC4Y 0DZ

www.johnmurraypress.co.uk

John Murray Press, part of Hodder & Stoughton Limited
An Hachette UK company

The authorised representative in the EEA is Hachette Ireland, 8 Castlecourt
Centre, Dublin 15, D15 XTP3, Ireland (email: info@hbgi.ie)

For my parents, my grandparents, my sister, my almosts

(Portraits unfinished / Later)

Later, a portrait of water. Portraits of black shine and
green and the screaming. Portraits of spades, a forest,
bones, voices of bones, cracked loss and caves. Portraits of
clawing back to the ghosts, and back to the caves and the
risk-lines and shine-screams because they are the sound
of the truth through long nights. Portraits of touch and
briefest music; portraits of threadbare hope and collapse.
Later, all these portraits. The wreck.

Part I

Portrait #1
The haunted

This is the portrait of who she used to be. She was a daughter – or rather, she was almost a daughter, because that was just the way things were – and she had always known what kind of cursed place she lived in, to a lesser or greater extent at different times.

She knew broadly, for instance, that her own mother's grandmother had been sent to the region from a better, cleaner city, in the west of the country and years ago. This was where the story ended: this great-grandmother was dead now and had always been dead, thick in the layers of mothers and past things. She had always been dead but did have something to do with the other woman who lived alone and had no family to visit her on weekends, so that the almost daughter's family came instead. They had brought her bread, because that was all she asked for, along with potatoes and cheap cabbageheads and onions. The lonely woman was not dead then but very old and had no whole teeth at the front of her mouth. She presumably had teeth at the back of her mouth, but the almost daughter had always avoided being close enough to be able to check, as doing so caused her a vague, pulsing nausea. On the days when the lonely woman spoke too much, the almost daughter could imagine the saliva pooling and foaming in the throat the voice was coming from, and the sensation would then spread out to her own throat. The room the woman lived in smelled of bare skin, and the onions. There were also days the family had come when the woman did not speak at all, or was howling or was not even dressed.

The almost daughter was aware that, like her mother's mother's mother, the old woman had also come from the city further west, and had not necessarily chosen to come. She knew that the place the women had ended up in, or had been sent to – the place that was her own town now – had not been a proper town at the time. The schools that she and her brother attended, and also the factories, and the apartment they lived in, had somehow not existed yet. It was difficult to think a lot about this, but the only reason the buildings were now there and solid, and were full of real things like noise and the lifts, was that people like her mother's mother's mother and maybe the lonely woman had been sent and not allowed to return. These people had had to remain for so long that all the blocks and lamp posts and the schools had been built and eventually had become a town. If the almost daughter sometimes did think about this, despite the difficulty and despite the fact that she generally had other things to think or not think, there really must have been a huge number of people sent from wherever else and not let back, if a whole life-sized town had ended up being built. At the same time, if so many people had been sent and then had not been allowed to go back, there must have been something and someone to keep them there, and the something must have been very large and strong, and the someone must have been many people, too. Then there was the question of why they had been sent, and why they were not permitted to go back, and this was where things were even harder to keep hold of. In any case, if it had been important and worth thinking so much about, surely someone would have said it all out loud by now.

But there was also the matter of the haunted fields where the athletics contests were held each year. For the almost daughter's brother this seemed less of a problem, as he was usually actually taking part, in either the long-distance lap run or the hurdle race. One year, he came second in both. The almost daughter was never selected for an event, except once when an error had been made in the high jump and a girl with exactly the same name as hers had qualified, but the error had fortunately been corrected before she had had to sprawl over the pole. Every remaining year, the almost daughter cheered, for her brother and for their school's other contestants, so it happened that she inevitably heard what the students from other regions said about the fields, in between their own phases of only cheering and shouting. They were the ones who said the word *haunted*, and sometimes said *labour* and *detained* and the other words. They were the ones who pointed to the blunt rows of what had indeed unmistakeably been *barracks*, before they boarded their buses and left again.

So of course the almost daughter had guessed, though equally naturally, she already knew. Clearly, everybody else knew as well, because why would she – just one boring, almost-person – be special in her guessing or knowing? Still, knowing was slightly different from speaking. Knowing was slightly different, even, from thinking. She sat at the table for dinner every evening with her brother, and with her mother, and her father if he was back from the gas plant, and they discussed when they would visit the lonely woman and bring her the vegetables in bags, until the day they stopped and did not go. The television was always bright and they turned the volume up or down, and they knew and their lips moved on and on. Her own almost face, in a portrait of before.

Portrait #2
Tops of heads

In this portrait, there is an actual portrait. It is the portrait that appeared in the lift in the section of the building the almost daughter lived in, the week before the strange time began with Oksana, the new and wild girl at her school, and all the things that were hidden under other things. It was with her father that the almost daughter first saw the portrait in the lift. There was no immediate logical connection to Oksana.

Her father swore quietly, into his breath. It was not an angry kind of swearing. The mirror in the lift was as scratched and hazed in the corners as it always was, but the portrait of the president was glistening. His skin looked taut-polished and the glass shined it further. The almost daughter's father repositioned himself but there was nowhere he could stand where he was not facing either his own reflection or the portrait.

It's a prank, he said. It's some kind of joke.

The almost daughter shrugged because this was what she did when she was not sure which words to say.

It'll be gone tomorrow, either way, said her father.

The next morning, the portrait was very much still there. The almost daughter stepped into the lift with her brother. There was a stain now on the portrait below the nose, where a straight moustache had been added in marker pen, and partially wiped away again.

What the hell, said the almost daughter's brother. He did not attempt to angle himself to not be looking directly at the portrait.

It's a joke, said the almost daughter. She told him that this was what their father had said.

Her brother asked what else their father had said.

Nothing, really, said the almost daughter. He said it was a joke, or a prank.

Her brother looked like his face was deciding whether it should be laughing or not. He took a photograph of the portrait with his phone. He started to take one of himself and the almost daughter in front of the portrait as well, but then he dropped his arm down instead. He deleted the original photograph he had taken.

Fuck, he said. Whenever they get caught, it won't be a joke for the imbeciles who thought of it.

The almost daughter shrugged and her brother moved his hands in and out of his pockets until they reached the sound like a sigh at the ground floor. Outside, as usual, the sky was still dark and so it was impossible to see his eyes. When they met his friend by the concrete steps of the old Palace of Creativity and Youth, and for all the rest of the way to school, he said nothing.

10

The almost daughter saw the portrait in the lift for the last time in the afternoon. She had begun to consider taking the stairs, even past the seventh floor, which stank most, because this would avoid being fixed inside the lift with anyone who might get in as well. At the same time, just as she realised she was calculating this, her thumb had automatically pressed the button, and a strange small section of her mind was less reluctant to find out what might happen if someone did get in. This part of her mind was faintly electric.

At the fifth floor, less than halfway up, there was the jolt-stop that meant the doors would open. Her strange segment of excitement drained back down the shaft.

The almost daughter only knew the woman who entered from seeing her inside the lift, which on all other days, without the portrait, was the same as never properly seeing her at all. The almost daughter would not have been able to recall if she lived on the fourth or the fifth or the sixth floor. She lived somewhere in the blur of the middle and nothing more.

The woman looked past the almost daughter to the portrait. The moustache, the almost daughter saw, had been redrawn, and rewiped, and words around the face had been added, and these had also been scrubbed out again or crossed through. There was a hair-crack in the glass in the bottom left-hand corner.

This was when the sound came that could easily have been something from the lift machinery. It could have been grinding cogs: it rasped and smacked.

The woman had spat. It had come from her throat. She turned and stepped out to the corridor again, and the almost daughter watched the wet projection settle, and then separate. The longest trail seeped down the nose to the mouth. It pleated, and was undeniably mesmerising.

11

In the evening, the almost daughter's mother sat in her head-phones and spoke to the screen. The almost daughter often watched her doing this while she wrote out her homework or partially read the chapters that she was supposed to be reading. Her mother spoke at the screen and looked into the camera hole and the box beneath the camera hole showed the woman who was in Bristol in England and who her mother was actually speaking to. The woman in Bristol spoke in English and this was to help her mother speak in English. Sometimes, her mother did not speak in English, but said things slowly and blandly, as if to a pet, and this was to help the woman learn, in exchange. The woman in Bristol was the person the almost daughter's mother had found on a website for her brother, so that she would help him speak in English before he took his exams to go to univer-sity. When her brother had said that the idea was idiotic and that he could just as well watch videos and not speak to a stranger, her mother had spoken to the woman instead. It was usually when her father worked late at the gas plant. At first it had been once a month and now it was at least one evening per week.

It is like a play, her mother was saying, in English. No, not play, she said. She shook her head. She typed on the keyboard and then spoke back to the woman. Not play, she said. It is like a game. Like joke.

At night, the videos arrived. The usual ones that came from her class and also the parallel class at the school were of animals that spoke in dubbed voices, or of people pouring hot things or cold things down their necks, but the preview images of what had been sent now were very clearly something differ-ent. She clicked on the first of them without breathing. She could see that it showed the inside of a lift.

The camera had been placed above the doors, so that the view of the portrait opposite was clear, and the people who stepped into the lift came into the frame with the tops of their heads first. Some of the tops of the heads that shifted in immediately shifted out again. Some faced the portrait for just a few seconds, and then turned their backs on it so that their expressions could be seen, distorted slightly from the angle. Two boys laughed and raised their hands in a salute, and one of them punched the other and he fell into the corner and was laughing still, but looked tired or nervous. Two other boys looked tired but did not laugh. One woman with a baby said: Aha, and one man with a case on wheels next to another man said: Just disrespectful. Disgrace, is what it is.

No one spat and no one marked on moustaches, in any of the videos. The almost daughter clicked on each of them again to check, and it was then that it became properly clear that this was not the lift in her building. She realised this and simultaneously realised that this was utterly obvious, or should have been. The mirrors were different, and the buttons were different, and the acrylic of the flooring was differently stained. In one video there was no mirror at all, and in another there was a handrail made of dark wood. All of the lifts were different places, and the lift that would show her brother, and her mother, and her father, and the woman who had spat, and also herself, was not the lift in any single one of the videos.

She checked this just one more time, and then read the comments from the rest of her class. Most had only responded with images that were either the yellow faces or the eyeballs. Some had said: Haha, but none said: Hahahahaha. One said: Too far, and many said: Oh God, and the almost daughter's deskmate said: Oh no. Her friend, who sat in front, said: Okay, but like that man says, it's pretty disrespectful, no? After this more had said: Too far, and Fuck.

The almost daughter returned to the top of the messages. The first video was from the person she knew would have sent it, without knowing especially that she had made this prediction. The person was the new girl, Oksana, though the second and third and fourth were not from her. These were with messages that said that the clips were forwarded from older brothers and cousins.

The almost daughter could hear her own brother in the other room with the computer on. He would come back soon. It was close to 4:30. He was watching other videos that he shouldn't have been watching. She sent one of the yellow faces and tried to choose which one her brother would pick if his class had also been sharing the lifts, and if these were the videos he had been watching instead of the ones he deleted after watching. She thought of him checking through each of them as well, squinting to recognise their parents or himself, and biting the inside of his cheek flesh like she had.

And then people were sending ferrets and baths of ice again already, and the videos pushed up to the nothing of the phone. The face she sent was an open-mouthed one. There was no face for the mixed wad of spark and dread that had told her in a kind of whisper that the new girl would be linked to the portrait in some way.

Portrait #3
The woman with the cave inside her

This is the portrait of a woman with a cave inside her. In this portrait, the woman with the cave inside her is standing in the approximate centre of the room, and is wearing one sock on each of her scabbed feet. This is good. There is supposed to be one sock on each foot. Why is it good? It does not matter, maybe. What matters is that they are on her feet, one each.

If they are on, and one on each, and it is still the morning, there is a chance for order and calm. There is the possibility that she will, today, remember and have the force to slice things and boil them, or layer them inside the pan, which will not exhaust her even as she lifts it, and she will remember first the butter in the pan. There is of course no certainty – not at all. But the potential has formed, if she has reached this far, that she may in fact recall whether this is a day when the key-click is expected at the door, and that she thus may not be frozen by the click and wait for it to disappear. With the socks and this good start in the centre of the room, not stuck or falling or too close to the window, she will come to the door, and recognise the faces. There is, if not clarity, a distinctness in the socks. She will recognise the faces as people and not ghosts.

She will know the faces as people and not ghosts.

And then no. No. It is not good. She is checking now, and yes, she has done it again. What she has done again is she has failed again. What she has managed is not good after all, and she is the dirtiest failure herself, because look at the colours of these socks more attentively, if this is possible without falling forwards and down. This one on the side of the window, left or right or whichever it is, is the grey sock with the red at the top. On the other side, the left or right other side, the sock is grey but the kind of grey that knows that it once, in another life, was white. It has no red and no other colour. It smells. It smells of her own smell that she hates as much as she hates her own skin and wastage and hands. They are terrible, awful hands to have, and now she sees that she is not wearing other clothes. This is not good and it is not good, or worse, that she even thought that the socks were good. How could she have thought that? She is naked.

She is naked, apart from the two different greys. The one that was white in another life is the one that stinks most of all, and of her. Not in another life at all, just in its own life, but so long ago. She could try again to get dressed, of course, but what is the point? So far and long ago.

The woman with the cave inside her. Hacked inside her and scythed inside her. Gape and another day, another life.

16

Portrait #4
Below, and history

The portrait from the lift, or from all of the lifts, is certainly somewhere in this next portrait too, because it was still somewhere within the almost daughter on the day this is a portrait of: the day that Valya had already decided would change their lives irreversibly, and forever. What Valya was talking about would happen later, but first there was the man with the broken briefcase who came to the school and held up a photograph of a monument that did not actually show the monument. Valya meant her own life, and Elda's life, and inevitably also the almost daughter's life.

The man came when the wall bell had rattled for the lunch break and there was groaning and swearing when the history teacher said that everyone should stay behind. She said that it would only take ten minutes. Less, if I can help it, she said. The almost daughter moved to sit at Valya's desk because clearly this did not count as a lesson. When Elda saw, she brought her chair close as well. Valya said she was sure that whatever was coming would be fascinating, and yawned to show her slack welt of chewing gum.

The man placed the broken briefcase on the front desk and lifted out the photograph. It was not large, and only showed the river.

This is a scandal, said the man. I'm sure we can all see that this is a scandal.

What he said, while the history teacher stood with her arms across her chest at the back of the room, was that a monument had been built some years before to stand up out of the river, near the gas plant. The monument had then collapsed and fallen into the water and was no longer visible, or was nearly not visible. He said that sometimes the tips of parts of it could be seen in the summers when the river was low.

The history teacher asked if he was coming to the point. Someone in another row asked whose idea it had been in the first place to put a monument in a river.

The point is we've finally raised enough funds to restore it and rebuild it, said the man.

The almost daughter squinted at the photograph. The pieces that often stuck up out of the river, especially when they were frozen there in winter, were logs, or mesh, or metal piping and scraps. If some were parts of a monument, they were indistinguishable from waste.

I told you this would be riveting, said Valya. Elda laughed too much and the almost daughter stopped looking at the photograph and also laughed.

The man with the broken briefcase was still speaking. He was saying that if anyone was interested in helping with restoring the monument and some other projects, they would be very welcome to join in. There are decisions to be made, he said. Young people, of course, are particularly crucial. We're even thinking of opening a small museum alongside working on the monument, and we'd be very keen to have your ideas. Other towns have made progress and now it's our turn.

In the room, the sounds of other voices and chair scrapes were already louder than the sound of the man's voice. It was not in any way necessary for the history teacher to clap her hands to interrupt the man, but this what she did, with force. She paced to the front of the room again, where she said that there had not been any agreement that the man could talk about the museum. This was meant to be just about the monument, she said. That was what we were assured.

The man nodded. They're only ideas, he said. We're very much in the initial stages.

The history teacher took the photograph from the man and held it out towards the desks again. Well, my dear crucial young people, she said. The sweat patches under her arms were perfect semi-circles. You're all so very welcome to join our good friend on his noble mission, she said.

She slammed the photograph back into the broken briefcase and said that the class could be dismissed, and the half that were not standing already hauled up and began to move to the door.

I haven't said when our meeting will be, said the man.

The history teacher was outside the door and the corridor noise fused into the room. The man said quickly that a meeting would be held in the music room, after lessons had ended. He latched the clasps on the broken briefcase and tapped limply on the one that clearly would not fasten. He stared at the blackboard for a number of seconds. Valya said something about the teacher's hormones, and Elda laughed, very loudly, again.

The almost daughter raised her bag strap slowly. The weighted thing that was happening inside her was more and more like being a lift in its shaft. She was the lift and was bound by the mechanisms that were summoning her, heavily, to the floors with pressed buttons. She could not see who and what was waiting and needing her on each of the floors, but she knew they had a magnetic hold, and she had a dull, vague sense of their outlines through this pull. On one floor, there was simply something related to the expression on the man with the broken briefcase, whose glasses, in fact, were broken too, though not to the same overt degree. His expression was causing something similar to the feeling she had had when her brother's old stitched-face rabbit from when he was very small had split open. It had happened only a year before and he had said that he did not care at all, but he had gathered every one of the rice grains from inside and his lips had been tightly matted together.

On another floor, waiting equally patiently, though of course the lift itself could never know which waiting was any more urgent than another, there was the photograph of the monument itself, or rather the photograph not of the monument. There was its sunken and drowned-in oddness only. And on the same floor, or in any case a close one, there was the strained aggression of the history teacher, which might mean nothing or might mean much more. There was still the portrait, somewhere, as well, and there was the question of who might stay with the man and ask him something, or even go to the meeting. It would not necessarily be Oksana, the new girl. It might be, but it could also be someone else. Finally, or

20

as finally as she could tell, there was the prospect of avoiding what Valya had decreed would change their lives so drastically, that afternoon. The almost daughter had not concretely been looking for a way to avoid this so far, but now that the prospect was there, it had a shape.

The almost daughter was suspended in the shaft. It had never been clear at all to her how any lift decided which floor to visit first when the buttons were pressed at exactly the same moment. The experiments she and her brother had conducted, years ago now, had never been conclusive.

In the corridor, her mouth opened smoothly, not a lot like the doors of a lift, but a little.

Maybe we should go to his meeting, just for fun, she said.

Elda and Valya, just ahead of her, both stopped. Elda's eyes flicked straight to Valya's.

Just for fun, said the almost daughter. Just to do something, for once.

Valya turned around completely and placed her palms on the almost daughter's shoulders. She asked if she was high, or possessed, or just an idiot.

Or all of the above, said Elda.

The almost daughter shrugged. Just for fun, she said again.

If you're telling me you don't even remember what we're doing after school today already, said Valya. Then go ahead and dig up the scummy river or whatever it is instead. Feel free.

Elda, in the shrill voice, repeated that she could feel free.

The almost daughter laid her hands over Valya's hands, both of which were still on her shoulders. It was difficult to make the shrug conspicuous with the hands there. I'm joking, she said. Calm down. I'm joking.

21

And then at the table in the hall by the kitchens, which was one of the tables near the radiator pipes because of how late they had been to arrive, and the almost daughter's hair was static and confining, Elda tried to eke out the mocking further, and Valya was plainly bored and had moved on. She was reminding them of the significance of the day still to come, and the potatoes tasted like soil or rain, and the man with the broken briefcase and his photograph was still somewhere close by. He had to be: he was in another classroom, or else he had already given up and was walking across the cement outside the school. Or someone – whoever, as it really could be anyone, and the new girl Oksana was just one example – was saying that they would come, first to the meeting, and then to help with everything that was trapped beneath the river's dead grey skin.

Portrait #5
On posture

This is the portrait of another almost thing, because the people from the modelling agency, it turned out, were not exactly people from the modelling agency. They were not the people who chose the girls who might become models and might be famous, which was what Valya had thought and said they would be. This was what her cousin had said they would be. Valya's cousin had been to see the people who chose at an event in another town, although she in the end had not been chosen. Valya had said she had been very close, and also that a man who rented out billboards to the people from the modelling agency had bought a space for his daughter on the list of the top twenty girls or top ten girls that rightfully had belonged to the cousin. She had said that the daughter of the man who rented out the billboards had a face like a goose.

The people who came to the school that day, instead, were people who gave information about the agency and collected money from anyone who wanted to go to the events with the people who did do the choosing.

It's called a casting, said the tall woman not exactly from the agency. But of course the numbers have to be limited even before you reach the casting. That's why there's the entrance fee.

The other person was a man in a suit. And it's not just that, you see, he said. You need to be really, properly prepared. It's no use just turning up as you are. If you're honestly going to be serious about it, we need to see that you're committed.

The woman explained that this was why there was a first entrance fee, to be paid immediately, and a second one in two months' time, to be paid if the participants had properly prepared and wanted to continue to the casting.

Did your cousin mention it would cost so much? said Elda. I don't remember you saying that.

Valya said that it was an investment. That's how you have to see it, she said. Think how much you could make back in just one job.

It's called a shoot, said Elda.

Or a job, said Valya. They say that too. And anyway, it does make sense that they need to be sure they don't get swamped with cases that are completely hopeless.

The almost daughter could not tell if Valya was looking too much at her. Elda was definitely looking at her. The tall woman and the man in the suit were showing photographs on the projector they had set up, and the almost daughter stared ahead at these. The poses of the girls with arched backs and stretched legs hovered over the rubber marks in the wall.

While the photographs continued, Valya said they would need to make a concrete plan. We'll have to cover everything in the two months we have, she said. Walking, clothes, body, and make-up.

And posture, said the almost daughter. This was something the tall woman had said while indicating the girls in the pictures.

We can meet once a week to train, said Elda.

Twice, said Valya. At least twice a week.

Elda said that this was what she had meant.

We could meet in here to do it, she said. My mother won't let us do it at ours and anyway she'll think we're training to be prostitutes. She doesn't really understand the difference.

The almost daughter thought then of two things. First that her mother probably thought the same, and then about the place she passed every day.

We can do it at the outdoor gymnasium, she said. Behind the old Palace of Creativity and Youth. No one ever uses it now and we'd have a lot more privacy there.

We'd freeze to death there, said Elda. That's insane.

If it's colder we'll look better in the photos we have to take for the portfolio, said the almost daughter.

Valya said that it was not a bad idea, and Elda said it was it worth considering.

The almost daughter added together the money she had inside her pencil case and in the mouse purse she kept at the bottom of her bag, and had enough, she concluded, more or less. The last girl in the photographs looked very, very cold.

On the rectangles of cement outside the school, Valya said that she would try to decide on something for their first training session. She said that Elda and the almost daughter could bring their own ideas as well, but that of course she did have slightly more experience, given what her cousin had reported back to her.

Your cousin who didn't actually get chosen, said Elda, and Valya said again that she had been very close.

And it's also how she met her boyfriend, she said. The one with the motorbike that came from Japan.

While Valya was describing the helmet that the boyfriend had bought with the cousin's name on it in red, the almost daughter was looking at her watch. It was an hour and a quarter since lessons had finished. Additionally, if she looked up again towards Valya, and seemed to be looking at her but looked past her, the lights in the music room might still be on. It was the same strange tugging in her mind shaft again, snagging on her to pay attention to Valya, but also doing the strange, deep things with the monument she had never even seen. It was mad because if she had not seen it, it was not even the monument itself but just the idea of it that was lurking so much. It was only an old and broken squat of stone, and only the very tips of it at that, but then there was also what was underneath, like having things to say but not knowing how, or having things to ask but never doing it properly. The lights in the music room – yes – were still on.

I forgot something, said the almost daughter. I left something in the bag with my indoor shoes.

She waited for Valya or Elda to ask what it was that she had left behind. Valya was still showing the size of the printed letters on the helmet in the air. It was Elda who said that they could not really wait. It's already getting late, she said.

If Elda and Valya walked together and without the almost daughter to the tram stop where they each got onto their separate lines, Valya might change her mind about the outdoor gymnasium. Elda might think of a better idea. The two of them might also rank the girls who had paid the first part of the entrance fee: they might decide on their top twenty, or top ten, and the almost daughter could imagine them deliberating. On the other hand, they would do this anyway, and without her, at some later point if they did not now.

I'll only be ten minutes, said the almost daughter.

Let's just say we'll see you tomorrow, said Elda.

Portrait #6
Backs of heads

The music room was emptier than the gymnasium had been, and there was no projector, and the man with the broken briefcase was not there. From outside the door, the almost daughter could not hear the words that were coming from any of the mouths that were moving inside. A boy from her brother's year group was sitting on the lid of the piano with his feet on the stool, and his mouth was moving most of all. The heads that were turned to him were backs of heads and only some were recognisable. Even if they did seem recognisable, they might turn around and still be wrong. The back of Oksana's head, for instance, did in all likelihood seem to be recognisable. The number of other students who had black hair that was rippled and also looked purple under certain lights was not an especially high number at all. It was zero, or at least it had been for some time, but of course it was always possible that someone else had chosen the same dye in the meantime. It was not probable, plainly, but it was possible.

The almost daughter blinked. The boy on the piano was doing something with his fingers that was different from what he was doing before, and his mouth was also doing something new. He was looking directly through the glass, at her. He was beckoning for her to come inside with his fingers, and the backs of heads were turning now as well.

She raised her hand to create a sign that would say she was only passing by and was on her way to somewhere else. There were all kinds of gestures to communicate this, surely. The hand stalled in the air for a moment and then pushed forward on the door.

Better late than never, said the boy on the piano. He pointed to one of the chairs in the skewed circle with his foot. Although we're basically already done for today, he said.

One of the heads that had turned and did not have the black, jagged hair that was also purple stood up and came towards her with a clipboard. The almost daughter remained in the doorway.

Just put your name here if you're interested, said the girl with the clipboard. We're having another meeting soon. We've not really decided anything yet.

The almost daughter did not take the uncapped pen. I wasn't really coming for the meeting, she said. I actually just thought I might have left something here.

The girl with the clipboard looked back at the boy on the piano and raised one eyebrow at him.

It's not a marriage certificate, he said. It's just a name.

We're not even starting with the monument, said the girl. We're only going to be talking about an exhibition and maybe a website.

29

The almost daughter took the uncapped pen with the hand that had pushed the door on its own. She passed it to the other hand and laid it on the clipboard.

I was really just looking for my scarf, she said.

The girl with the clipboard rolled her eyes. She said she had not seen a scarf in the room and sat back down on the chair she had left. The boy on the piano began speaking again, not looking at the almost daughter. The heads became backs of heads again.

Not all of the heads became backs of heads again. The one with the black hair that was also purple stayed turned around for a few seconds more.

You can come without signing, as well, said Oksana, from under the hair, which jumped as she spoke. You can be a free agent if it suits you better. And by the way, she said. I think – well, it looks like you might have found your scarf already.

She winked before turning, which made the hair twitch again, and the almost daughter was in the corridor, and then moving, not running, but certainly more than walking. The temperature of her neck was heated and conscious as she reached to touch the wool of her stupid, too-wound scarf.

She squinted to check if she might see Valya and Elda still ahead on the way to the tram stop, maybe deciding to pay for a proper modelling school after all, without her. There was at least one, though in another part of the town. It would be Elda who would suggest it first, and Valya would say it was unfair not to tell her, and Elda in some way would make the discussion about her mother and the illness she had again, which made things hard for her and meant she had to be supported,

30

and being supported meant whatever she wanted it to. The almost daughter did not squint for long.

She took the shortcut that was not much of a shortcut, but was more interesting and went down to the river. Then she was not on the shortcut any more, but still following the low iron railings that divided the road and the embankment from the river. She reached the point that was opposite the gas plant, where her father would be at that very moment, and between them there seemed to be only water. Between her and anyone, all it looked like on the surface was the water.

I can be a free agent, she could say to the tips of the monument if she stopped for long enough, even if she could not quite see them and even if she would not quite say it with her voice. I can do whatever I want, she would say.

Portrait #7
The woman with the cave inside her

The woman with the gape-cave inside her is stuck again. This portrait is an empty frame and is also a portrait of a balcony. She knows she is not meant to go out to the balcony and the woman who comes with the two lazy children has explained the reason several times. She knows there is a reason and the frame of the reason is something that she can feel out and reach to, but she cannot make out what is held within the frame.

The fact is that on the balcony, out there, the air must be fresh and clean and bright, or at least it must be fresher and brighter than inside. Inside is the smell that she knows is herself. The smell is locked in the choked air inside and it is locked inside her skin even more. Outside on the balcony, where the frame-reason tells her she is not supposed to go, there is the yellow clouded plastic and the metal top rail and the textures that are simply not the inside textures. There are the wires and cars and buses to look down on, and windows to look over to with lights on or off, which all mean that people are moving and choosing things: deciding where they want to be, and going there. They are not people who are locked in their skins.

She keeps the frame of the reason not to go on the balcony in one of her hands – it is probably the left – and uses the other to unbolt the door. The scrape sound calls out for the reason at first but then it becomes a weak grunt and gives up. It tells her to keep pulling and step out.

The cold really is a fresh bite: it is a flavour. It stings at her and enters and is all around her, like a sudden, total kind of waking. Her lungs glow wide with the taste of it and are alive, so that maybe – maybe – she is live enough too.

How long is she standing, inhaling, before it withers? It does not matter how long it is and how blazing the breath has been, because what matters is now: she is looking down. Not to the street and vehicles and the choices, but before that, to the grill-grate that is the floor of the balcony. It is a grill-grate which means that it is mostly open space, and even the not-space parts of it are thin. Rusting and pathetic, says the voice of the woman who comes with the watching and lazy children, and this is the reason to fill the frame. Needs repairing and replacing completely, says the voice, but we both know that's unlikely to happen. This is why it is forbidden here and dangerous, and can she hear the rust flakes curling off like paper? Is it something she is imagining or not? If these are her last moments, before the grill floor splinters, and she plummets after all of this, at least her lungs will have been free one last time.

She inches – how long for, again, cannot be counted – backwards over the spindles of the grill-grate. If they break, if she falls. If she falls, if they break. If she breaks. Would it be slow or sharp?

The only thing to do back inside is to find the papers that will make her feel better. They will make her feel calm, or soft, and on the ground again, for a little while at least and are the only things that do this. Not just papers – what are they? Letters. And a photograph. The photograph of the face that will make her feel safer. They are somewhere. She keeps them hidden, just in case, even if she is not sure in case of what. She hides them well every time. She puts them back. She hides them from the woman and the lazy children except that once or maybe twice she did not hide them but she held them out and screamed things. They are hidden but now they are too well hidden. If she could remember where it was she hid them she would have them in her hands this moment.

So she is stuck with her hand on the bolt, now silent. The face does not come without the photograph, not any more, and can't make her feel safe. It used to come without the photograph. It may be behind the mirror with the brass hook, or in one of the envelopes in the corner on the chest there, but these places are exhaustingly far away from where she is crouched by the balcony bolt. Is the woman with the lazy children coming today? Her key-click for turning. That woman and her children. That woman – that ghost of the ghost of the ghost. Might she know where the photograph is? But hidden.

Portrait #8
Under fur

On Saturday, there was school in the morning, but Valya sent a message to say she was not going, and Elda immediately replied. She was not either. The almost daughter turned the pillow over and tried to stop her mind from remembering how much it was a lift in a shaft. She watched a video on her phone of a woman from an agency that was different from the one that would be holding the casting. There's just something unique about this region, she said. The girls have the clearest skin, maybe from the cold, and strong faces and exquisite bone structure. It's partly the history, of course, she said. People ended up here from so many different places. But the point is that their faces and bone structure are so strong, exotic, even, in plenty of cases, and it's a beauty that is striking and unusual. The woman used the word for strong seven more times.

When the video ended, the almost daughter could hear her mother preparing to leave. She rolled shut the drawer that had keys inside it, and if she had been taking the onions and roots to the lonely woman, like before, the almost daughter could have got up and joined her. A version of her could and would have joined her mother, even if it was just to be moving and not thinking.

Her brother appeared after midday in the kitchen with his friend and not alone. The friend, Yevgeniy, was not the worst of his friends, but was also not someone the almost daughter wanted to have in the kitchen on a Saturday, especially when there were things it would have been useful to try to hear her brother's opinion on. It would have been useful to hear what he really thought, which was hard enough in any situation, but impossible if Yevgeniy was there. His opinions voiced in front of his friends were not the same as his real opinions, because nor were hers in front of anyone else.

When her brother asked why she hadn't been at the school, she said she had but that her last lesson had been cancelled. So I just got back here early, she said.

When you lie your nostrils flare out, said her brother.

Yevgeniy snorted.

It's true, said her brother. Look. You can see them.

The almost daughter pinched her nose with her hand and then released it. It doesn't really matter anyway, she said. She cut a cube of cheese from the plate in front of Yevgeniy. Because I'm going to be an actress, she said.

Yevgeniy snorted again. A what? he said.

An actress, said the almost daughter. It's not like I really need school for that.

Her brother opened the fridge door and looked inside without moving. Don't you have to be attractive to be an actress? he said.

Yevgeniy's laugh this time burst breadcrumbs. Sorry to break it to you, he said.

I said an actress, said the almost daughter. Not a model.

Same difference, said Yevgeniy.

Her brother turned. He's right, he said. He was holding more cheese and not looking at her. They're all whores or at best they're escorts, he said.

The almost daughter watched Yevgeniy, who was still snorting but also seeming as if he was no longer sure how long he should continue.

You would know, she said. You both would.

When her mother returned, her face looked emptied. Before, when she had gone to see the lonely woman, she had used to come back with the stinking and curling old onions and cabbages that she must have replaced. If she had brought them back this time, the almost daughter could have taken the bag and its sour smell to the garbage chute. She would have tipped each of the lumps into the void in turn. She would have kept count and if she ended on an even number, she would have asked her mother about what she thought of modelling and escorts and whores, and maybe other things as well.

Instead, her mother was making the salad that was fish underneath sliced potatoes and eggs. It was the salad that was called a herring in a fur coat.

Your favourite, said her mother, and she nodded.

In the bedroom, when her brother and Yevgeniy had gone out, she checked the difference between escorts and whores.

Whores were something obvious, but escort was just a word that was similar to whore but was somehow sleeker and less dirtied. Her research suggested that she was right. Escorts were paid more. They went to parties and hotels. She watched a video of a woman who said she loved her job and was proud of it and had once been to Paris on a plane for a week-end for six thousand dollars. The pages that showed whores and prices were awful, and the women and girls had thick, sad-slack buttocks. The pages for escorts often did not have photographs, or if they did they sometimes only showed eyes, behind long hair or through black and silver masks that were for balls. It was easy enough to imagine Yevgeniy squinting and muttering at all of the photos, and it was easy to imagine her brother doing this too.

The way her father ate the salad was to cut straight through to the herring and eat it first. He did this quickly, while talking about a colleague at the gas plant who was either too aggressive or not aggressive enough, and watching the news on the television as he spoke. He kept his eyes on the screen as he forked through to the fish, as if he knew exactly where it was and always would be.

Her brother piled each forkful he took with an equal proportion of each of the layers. There was potato and egg and cubed carrot and peas and the herring every single time, in the same order and hardly mixed at all, and he could also manage this without looking down.

Her mother left the herring until last.

What happened to the almost daughter that evening was that she could not remember how she always ate the salad. It was ridiculous, and also ridiculous that she was thinking about it, like suddenly noticing the rhythm of breathing and not being able to stop and feel normal. She could not eat the salad in a way that did not feel artificial and conscious. It was absurd: there was something clearly very wrong with her, though perhaps it was more wrong that she actually cared. She tried to watch the screen and listen to her father and the way that they melted together like they always did. She tried to be automatic, like the others.

The result was that she was keeping the herring hidden under the layers as long as she could. Every time she thought it was about to be uncovered, she found a way to keep it under. Her eyes glanced down and checked so she was not automatic. Of course, it was impossible to hide it forever, but when she reached it she did manage not to look at it at all. She was like her father and her brother at last again. She could watch the men on the news and know where everything was on her plate without seeing it.

It was when she was brushing her teeth in the evening that her brother came in, spat, and spoke again.

If you went to that presentation or whatever it was at school about the modelling, you're basically already a whore, he said.

She said she had no idea what he was talking about. She splashed his hands and then his neck with water, and he folded his towel into two triangles and cracked it like a whip in the air.

I'm serious, he said. If it turns out – if I find out you're doing that filth.

He raised his arm into a fist and shook it, but serious was the last thing he was. There was no point now in asking what he thought about the monument, and the man with the broken briefcase and history, even without Yevgeniy there.

Portrait #9
The woman with the cave inside her

The woman with the cave gouged inside her is lying in the bed that is now dry and clean. It will be clean for however long it takes for her smell to ruin it and poison it again.

In the morning, she and her bed were not clean and she was doing things that were not clean and true. She was pretending that she had always been awake. Or at least, that she had been awake for longer than the moments between the knock at the door and the key-click and seeing the atrocious, worst ghost there. Of course, it was not really the atrocious ghost who had come to the door and let herself in, because she never came – she could not come – but instead it was the ghost of the ghost of the ghost. When was the last time she had come? The ghost of the ghost of the atrocious ghost: who came out of pity or guilt, or what? In any case, she had come again. She had a paper bag of the vegetables that were hard and in hot water would turn to be soft, and she placed it next to the bag from the last time. She had not brought either of the two lazy children.

The ghost of the ghost of the atrocious ghost was speaking more than on other days. She was talking but she was bent to the sink, because she was scraping and scrubbing at something. The woman with the cave inside her remembers all her scraping and scrubbing.

We'll get this looking brand new, was what the ghost of the ghost of the ghost was saying over water. Brand new and all clean and then it's your turn next, don't worry.

If the woman with the cave inside her could open her eyes enough and scour their grit away, she was sure that she could seem to be awake. And she could flatten her hair still and pull her face out of creases, and the ghost of the ghost of the atrocious ghost might perhaps not see the bedsheets at all. At this point, the woman with the cave so wretched inside her had still thought this was possible.

Oh, said the ghost of the ghost of the ghost. Not again.

The ghost of the ghost of the atrocious ghost moved to the bedsheets and peeled them back. She still had her hands in the thick rubber gloves, like the woman with the cave inside her was also a mess in the sink and curdled.

Revolting and curdled, thinks the woman with the cave inside her now. Yes. Curdled. Curdled and curdles every single thing she touches.

But still there was something, while the ghost of the ghost of the ghost was prying the sheets away and holding them stretched out far from her, that the women with the cave inside her wanted to ask her to help with, was there not? There was something she had been looking for and needed, in order to curdle just a brief instant less. There was something to ask the ghost of the ghost of the ghost to help her find again. There was something.

Still the ghost of the ghost of the ghost was talking and talking over the wet-spoiled sheets, and the woman with the cave inside her could not hold space for the thought of what it was that she had needed to ask. Was it? Was it not? Wasn't it to find? The ghost of the ghost of the atrocious ghost was also speaking of finding. But not the right thing. A different thing she had found, on paper. The ghost of the ghost of the ghost said more and more, and then her rubber hands were on the shoulders of the woman with the cave inside her.

Come on, said the ghost of the ghost of the ghost. It's definitely your turn now.

In the dark of the bathroom she talked even more, and the woman with the cave inside her had to hate her skin freshly as the glove hands uncovered it. The ghost of the ghost of the ghost was talking about clean things, and then what she was saying changed.

You have to wipe it over and start again, she said. You can't just keep staring at the dirt times of the past.

And she was talking about the papers she had found, which were not what the woman with the cave inside her needed. A sort of leaflet, she said. But not very well made. Clearly they've been into the schools as well. They're organising meetings and who knows what else.

I mean, it was in the bin, she said. A good sign that they won't get involved, of course. But then on the other hand, whoever it was still took the leaflet in the first place, and brought it back. And I've found them twice now, as well, remember.

The woman with the cave inside her was almost ready to ask the ghost of the ghost of the atrocious ghost to slow. If she slowed, the woman with the cave might follow. If the ghost

42

of the ghost of the ghost was caring so much about the paper things, it maybe was important to the ghost herself, too. And this was where there was close to a connection.

I'm just worried that one of them might be persuaded, said the ghost of the ghost of the atrocious ghost. Why would they have brought the leaflets back, and twice? Whoever it was. He might be, at least, she said. I think she's less likely to want to get involved. Either way, I just want them to be safe. I know, and I know, but I want them to be safe.

There was warm, weak water over skin, and it was true: it was making the woman with the cave inside her feel cleaner, purer, looser, soft. It would let her soon, here, sleep again. It was hard to hold any other part of thought, and hear the ghost of the ghost of the ghost. I know, she was saying. But it's just better not to dig. But it was hard and too slipping away to attach to what the ghost of the ghost of the ghost had been saying, about the two she must be talking about and what they might or should or should not be digging. The lazy boy and the lazy other one: the other one with her ghost-green eyes and the haunt of her inside the eyes. Or instead they should be cleaning over. Wiping fresh. Too lost, too slipping away in warm water. Lost the thing she was wanting to ask for.

The woman with the cave cut inside her was washed and dried, and quiet. Quiet.

But here in the bed and now she remembers, solidly, what she wanted to ask. About the photograph of the atrocious ghost. And the letters. Where? Behind the—? Under the—? Where. The ghost of the ghost of the ghost might have known, if there is anyone still to know.

She is dry and dry, and then at some point, not so dry.

Where and find and never find.

Portrait #10
Strengths

This is the portrait of metal rings and chains and worn-in bars and moving parts that made up the asymmetrical machines at the outdoor gymnasium. This is the portrait of Valya on a balance beam, Elda on something like a bicycle with no wheels, and the almost daughter lying on her back with her knees raised, on a tilted steel sheet that once had been the roof of a car. Every time she straightened her legs flat, they pushed away a rusting disc that was attached to an oversized hinge above, itself attached to further weighted discs. The pushing through her legs was exhausting, but effective.

There was another outdoor set of machines located further from the river, with larger and newer equipment that was not welded from lost pieces of vehicles and engines. The other, new place was where real bodybuilders trained. They were vast, sweat-slicked men in sleeveless vests and damp headbands, and they trained outside in summer and in winter and spat into the snow when they grunted to each other about the young, soft people who paid for indoor fitness clubs.

The almost daughter had seen them there, and she therefore knew that the outdoor gymnasium behind the old Palace of Creativity and Youth, which had been her suggestion and so her responsibility, was substandard, which could count against her, but was also a place they would most likely be alone, which was the part that she had emphasised to Valya. Her brother and two friends of his had met there, for a time, along with other straggled groupings clearly not part of the true bodybuilding circle. One of the friends had torn his forearm open on one of the protrusions of jagged iron, and the three of them had stopped meeting there after that. So they would have the place to themselves, and for free. The almost daughter did not know which precise machine had ripped the skin. Quite plainly, there were several contenders available.

Elda had appeared to be assessing one of them as she reached out and then retracted her arm when they had first arrived. Is this really what we're looking for? she had said. It's kind of disgusting, if we're honest, no?

The almost daughter had tightened her breath. But—

For God's sake, Valya had said. We're here now.

The almost daughter had relished the rolled eyes. They were rolled for her, but said more about Elda. Valya had provided instructions on which of the machines were suitable for them to use, and which were too complicated or too manly.

We don't need to look like pumped gorillas, she said. It's just about toning and definition.

She assigned which of the pieces of equipment in the staggered oval they would each begin with, and set the stopwatch on her phone. In the middle of the oval, cleared of greyed snow, was a statue of three angular athletes on a podium. One of them was missing a nose, and one of them was missing his whole head. The place where his neck ended was smooth and rounded, and popular with both the grey crows and sparrows. The almost daughter used this centrepiece of severed strength as the fulcrum of her circuit around the machines.

And now, on the board with her legs pressing and folding back, she had established a deliberate rhythm: with each push, she felt a little more power. She was ramming away words like Whore and Escort, and the sad girls' faces on the pages she had found, and in turn she was drawing closer to herself the approval of Valya, and the chance of rolled eyes. She could drive off or summon what should be large and strong in her mind as it suited her, and what should stay only faint and small. She could even push away the monument and everything attached to it, back to where it came from and unseen.

Change! shouted Valya, all too soon, and the almost daughter climbed down and progressed to the left, onto the parallel bars.

After three completed rounds of the machines, Valya motioned for a gathering around the maimed statues. She distributed two notebooks from inside her bag and kept a third on her lap to demonstrate. On the first ruled page within each cover, a photograph had been printed and glued over the lines.

They're all different, said Valya. They're for inspiration.

They were different but did not look so different, and looked the same as the girls that the tall woman from the modelling agency, or not really from the agency, and the man in the suit had displayed at the school. They looked the same, very nearly, as the whores and escorts on the pages, but with the whole of their bodies and generally more clothing. Valya said that the girl in the almost daughter's book had been chosen from a town just sixty miles north, and was only fourteen when she was selected.

And now she's in New York and Milan, she said.

For the next twenty minutes, they watched a documentary of the glued girl in the photograph in Valya's book. She opened wide a wardrobe packed with shoes and said that this was just what she kept at home. I have my other dressing room at the studio, she said.

When she detailed her routine before her most important castings and magazine shoots, and said that she drank only tea and ate buckwheat, with no salt, for the twelve days before the event, the almost daughter pinched in her tongue. She had been close to laughing or to pausing the video and saying that this was over the top. It was like the push and pull on the press machine again, using her effort through her legs. She could control what to haul towards her, or banish.

So it was Elda who said: Twelve days? That's too far.

Valya shook her head. Not really, she said. Not if you really want it, anyway.

It really was a continuation of the rhythm, and a hauling of things into the right shapes and outcomes. At the end of the video, the girl's mother and grandmother were saying how proud of her they were. The mother had tears and the grandmother did not. The almost daughter towed in the correct things to say when Valya said that this would be them, too, one day, and she cast away the skulk of questions she had seen in the sparse teeth of the grandmother. They were the same sinking questions about escorts and whores, and what the point of it all really was, and they did not belong inside her.

Portrait #11
In beads

This is a portrait created by the almost daughter. It is a portrait she did not realise at the time was a portrait.

First, however, there was the woman in Bristol in England on the screen when she came into the apartment. The almost daughter had the notebook from Valya tight against her underneath her coat, and the plan was to slip it between the other books and folders that were wedged in her bag for school. The head in Bristol in England on the screen was partially blocked by her mother's head, in the room.

Her mother was telling the head in the square about the salad with the herring. She was explaining the translation of its name.

Or more accurately, it is herring under the fur coat and not in, she said. This is how we are calling it.

The woman in Bristol in England was laughing. Her lips were moving and the earphones took her words.

Yes, said the almost daughter's mother. Yes, I like it very much. You do not know, but I have made this salad just few days ago. It is because of a little of stress I am feeling. I make this salad when I am feeling stress in me.

There was a movement in Bristol in England like a question.

It is not a big and important stress, said her mother. It is just because of a thing that happens that I am feeling worry about.

No, not the elevator problem that I told you, she said. It is a new problem that happens now.

There was no reflection of the almost daughter's mother's face over the face of the woman in Bristol in England because the screen on the computer was better and less shiny than the screens her brother and Yevgeniy used to look at the pages of photos of girls.

There is a type of group, said the almost daughter's mother. Not a real association like in the cities and in some towns, but a small type of group, I think, that is wanting to—

She stopped to type and to look for words.

They want to dig in our history, she said. Dig, I think, or excavate. They are wanting to dig things that are down in our past.

The mouth in Bristol made shapes that were another question, or many questions.

Yes, said the almost daughter's mother. In many times yes but in our situation, no. It is not good. It is too dangerous to do this. It has happened before. They will—

She typed.

They will convince the young people, she said. They will convince the young people to dig and this will not be safe for them.

The woman in Bristol in England was producing more of her questions with her mouth and eyes, but the almost daughter's mother's head was shaking.

I do not want to think of this, she said. Now we will change our language, yes?

She began to speak in the loud, slow way, and asked the woman if the pen was on the table, and then if the books were on the shelf. The woman in Bristol took a long time to answer, and the almost daughter pretended to find whatever she had been searching for in the backpack.

In the bedroom, she did real searching. There was a box in the cupboard somewhere, still, that was packed with tubes of tiny metal beads. They had once been intended for making bracelets, but the almost daughter had never understood how to work the wiry loom they came with. Someone had given her the contraption one New Year when she was small, and she had imagined making perfect and well-aligned bracelets with it. Instead, she had always tied the threads incorrectly and dropped the beads like sawdust on the floorboards, initially by accident and then by throwing them. They had jammed beneath her fingernails like pieces of grit.

One night, at a time that was before she had a phone, she had been spinning a bottle cap on the bedstead. It skated out under the mattress and when she crouched to retrieve it, she found several of the miniscule beads as well. Something bulky and raged had been in her mind: she had been arguing with her brother about the bottle cap, and he had said that her front teeth were giant, and she had known that this might well be true.

It happened in a way that seemed fast, and maybe was, and soon she had arranged the tiny beads within the circle on the underside of the bottle cap. She located the box with the tubes of other beads, and filled in the remaining void. It was delicate and difficult but quieting. It was a portrait of how she felt, in colour and pattern and spiral, and in a way that no one else would understand. She was calm and concentrated and used glue and a toothpick to hold the beads in place when they were right.

Over time she had amassed a collection of the portrayals, proportional to the number of caps she claimed, and to the gravity of situations and thoughts that made her need the process.

When her father had stopped drinking beer, she had stopped. Or else she had stopped because once she had shown Valya the stack of caps underneath the bed, and Valya had said that it was probably a madness. It's like what they do in asylums, she said. Or serial killers, when they're children.

Now that her brother drank the beer, and neither of them bothered to collect the caps, it was easy to find an unbent one on his side of the room between his clothes. And when she did find the tubes of beads, she saw that somehow they were hardly empty. There was the glue and the toothpick beside them in the box.

As she guided the colours and formations now, or maybe as they guided something in her, she recognised quickly the mysterious release of being able to be both sure and unsure what represented what at the very same time. It was like words, but so different, and she could show her insides without having to know herself exactly what they were. She glued the pieces down. She hid the box again. The indents in the tips of her fingers were not from any specific bead that directly referred to anything: not to escorts or whores or Valya's questions, and not to the dangers and excavation either. Even if they did, no one else would know the code.

It was stupid, really, that she was playing with the beads again, and yet it was still a way to be slow and rest a brain for a small and closed while.

When her brother came into the bathroom later, and her mouth was a mix of fresh foam and her own slime, he stood behind her and fixed on her eyes in the mirror. He had been doing this increasingly often: he would enter, and usually he would only brush too, and warp his face into shapes in the mirror. It was something he had used to do when they were younger.

Mostly he gargled and did not say much. This time, he watched her before he reached for the tap.

Yevgeniy says he saw you after school, he said. At the old Palace of Creativity, or near there.

She blinked. I hope you pay your spies well, she said.

It just seems kind of weird, he said. No?

I'm creative, she said. I'm a youth.

Portrait #12
The woman with the cave inside her

When the woman with the cave inside her bursts into waking in the middle of a night, either one of two things happens.

The first is that the atrocious ghost comes, without even the photograph to bring her. But because she has come in the dark middle of a night, she is there in a crying way, in a screaming way, a pleading way, and the woman with the cave inside her is fully, drenchingly guilty and pinned. This is what almost always happens. Eyes and eyes and bright-dead eyes.

The second thing that can happen is that just for a moment, she remembers or believes that she has tried. She is guilty but not only guilty, and has tried. She did try to look for the atrocious ghost and tried to save her and tried to keep her, and then when she was too late and failed, she tried with the ghost of the ghost. She searched and searched for the ghost of the ghost, who had the same ached eyes as the ghost. And that was too late and so she tried with the ghost of the ghost of the atrocious ghost. And then there was the lazy ghost of the ghost of the ghost of the atrocious ghost. She gave her presents and treats when she was small and tried to sometimes speak and explain to her, except that she did not speak enough. She gave her the bicycle and the dresses and the wire thing, which was something to make jewellery with and was oddly expensive, close to as much as the bicycle. The ghost of the ghost of the ghost of the ghost had said she would wear the dresses for her, and would make her a necklace or a bracelet or anything, but then this became a promise like any other promise. It was nothing at all: it was another hole to fall through. The ghost of the ghost of the ghost of the ghost was just a lazy child with eyes that promised the ghost but were nothing of her, really.

Like this, the second path of burst-waking falls straight back into the first one again. The woman with the cave inside her is packed and drenched with only promises that cannot be kept and are just foretastes for the guilt. All kinds of them, all bloated and hurt kinds and there is nothing she can do about them now, in the middle dark of a ceaseless night. The ceaseless echo cave inside her.

Where are the letters? Where are they? And the eyes?

Eyes that made things closer, stronger.

Part II

Part II

Portrait #13
In March

There was a week and then another week, and the almost daughter went with Valya and Elda to the outdoor gymnasium twice in each week. Also twice each week, they met in Valya's stairwell, to study more videos and photographs and to practise posture, contours and faces. Whenever the almost daughter felt bored or weak, she pedalled harder or stood up straighter. She lengthened her neck and told her shoulder blades to meet. She copied the downcast smoked-eye expressions from the photos.

After the week and the second week, there was the day that happened in spring every year when men were supposed to give mimosas to women, and people sent messages about how women were special, and there was a banner roped in front of the school. The huge banner was the same as every year and said: We dearly love our mothers, sisters and wives. It had worn scratches in the corners and threads leaking from its cords.

There were no mimosas on the almost daughter's desk. This was fortunate, in several ways, though it also made Elda smirk across the room.

The almost daughter noticed and then decided not to notice that when she walked past the parallel class there were no mimosas on Oksana's desk either, and also that there was no Oksana at her desk. This was the case from the beginning of the day, but it was only after the morning break that she heard the things that were being said.

She went completely insane, said someone. Like just flipped.

She was screaming, apparently, said someone else. She hit two of the teachers who tried to stop her.

You'd think she'd be more into a day that says women are the centre of the world, said the boy who was one of the boys who had left mimosas on Valya's desk, with a note, and had said things that were like this before. If you know what I mean, he said. You know what I mean.

As they spoke and muttered more, predictions were assembling in the part of the almost daughter's brain that was pressed below the main part of it, which was copying the diagram from the geography textbook. When people were in trouble, they were sent to the director, and had to sit outside her office until she and the secretary were ready to see them. The seat outside the director's office was a hard brown chair like no other in the building. It seemed to be lower than any chair was meant to be.

They'll kick her out again, said someone. And didn't she only just get kicked out somewhere else?

But that was for— said someone else. Well, you know what I heard about that.

58

The almost daughter could not hear the rest, or equally had resolved that she would not hear.

There was something, though. Whether or not she had heard or cared, it was true that she needed to go to the bathroom. It was true that she had been there in the break, already, but this had mainly been to be of assistance to Valya, whose hair had curled too much in some places and in some places not enough. She had needed to stand over the sinks for twenty minutes until leaving, looking exactly the same, and had needed someone to be standing with her.

It would only take a second to go to the bathrooms on the third floor instead of the second floor, because the cubicles on the second floor stank worse, and to glance quickly.

Oksana was upside down on the chair. Her legs were straight against the back rest and the wall behind, and her back was flat on the hard seat part. Her elbows were strange at an angle on the floor.

I can see you, she said, although this seemed impossible. I can hear you which means I can essentially see you, she said. Plus there are my eyes in the back of my head.

The almost daughter had moved along the corridor and past the bathrooms and had not gone in. Oksana pivoted upright in one swift motion.

Oh, she said. Weird. It really was you I saw.

It was time to leave. For the almost daughter, it was undoubtedly time to turn and leave.

An ignition was sparking in Oksana's face.

You're still looking for that scarf, right? she said. What a bitch. Your scarf, to keep sneaking off like that. But then again, at least you're not about to be executed.

What made sense for the almost daughter to do now was to leave the corridor and go to the bathroom, or even better, to go straight back to the classroom.

Executed? she said to the chair.

Let's be honest, Oksana said. The only reason they wouldn't do it is because my bad blood would stain the carpets.

It was not time to go. It was long past time.

What was it you did? said the almost daughter.

Oksana's face parodied offended surprise. Is that the question you should be asking? she said. Shouldn't you ask what they did first to deserve it?

I— said the almost daughter.

Never mind, said Oksana. It doesn't matter anyway. It's all just a kind of diversion, really. Keeps them thinking that this is the only thing I care about.

She looked both sly and proud across her cheekbones.

I just pulled their banner down because it's so hypocritical, she said. And if it ripped on the way, it was clearly poorly made. And maybe also I just said or maybe shouted, what if you don't feel you're that kind of woman? What they say any kind of woman should be? Where's your special day if you feel like that?

The director's door could open at any second. What do you mean? said the almost daughter.

Oksana regarded her. But like I said, it doesn't matter, she said. Or it does, but it's to keep them off the scent, as well.

She checked sideways to the door, and then bent to her black bag. She emerged with a rubber-banded sheaf of folded paper.

Here, she said. Just have a look. You never know. It's to keep them distracted from this, in a way.

The almost daughter took the paper. She did not focus on it but was close to ninety per cent sure that she had seen the words *monument* and *campaign* already.

Although for me it's not all totally unrelated, said Oksana. But most importantly, either way, maybe you'll even finally find that scarf.

She winked.

She really winked, like before, and the almost daughter turned.

By the evening, she had crushed the paper to be very small and buried in her pocket. She had pulverised everything that had been said in the corridor and now it was the moment to throw it away – in the apartment, so that no one at the school would see. The paper, the words about the right kind of feeling, and the wink that was playing on repeat: wrung and strangled. The date and time and place on the paper, and the place was the most intriguing, slightly eerie thing, but none of this was significant because the paper was about to be thrown away. It would sit in the bin and be practically dead.

She crunched it one more time, and went into the kitchen. She opened the cupboard that was under the sink and shuffled the things at the top of the bin to ensure that the paper was sufficiently obscured.

And then – in the shuffle – another paper, identical. Screwed small in a different way, and also hiding. Just like her piece of paper, it said that the next meeting would be at the Palace of Creativity and Youth, and said *urgent*.

She kicked the cupboard shut, and it yelped.

Portrait #14
The woman with the cave inside her

The woman with the cave inside her is in the kind of soup again. A day that is soup is not the worst kind, but it is smudged and lagging and slugs around. It must be afternoon, or later, because of the direction of cars and because of what is left of last sun. However, this may also be a trick of the soup.

It is the soup that smothers what happens with the buzzer or that conjures the buzzer, even, out of nothing. It comes and why should it? It must be just the soup. Because the ghost of the ghost of the ghost, on days she comes, knows the numbers for the door at the bottom – and she has the key that clicks and so no buzzer. No buzzer like this sad steel insect.

So why the buzzer now? Who? And she is slowed. Hours or days or seconds are smeared before she reaches the pinprick holes of the wall-box, and so of course no one will be there now, if anyone was ever there, and not simply soup-born.

And when she presses and indeed there is someone there and the someone is breathing, straight through the box holes, she is so unbelieving that she also only breathes. More decades, or stretched, taut minutes and then—

Hello? she says. Who's out— Who's there?

Her voice is swamped in soup and the tone comes, a second metal insect and a sound of ending. It is the clearest and most decisive shape to penetrate the dense broth fog.

Still, she is drifted by its ripple to the balcony. Not to open – no, she remembers: danger and a falling floor – but she can look out here and down to check.

There. It must be. There she is.

Not the ghost of the ghost of the atrocious ghost, but smaller, quicker and less distinct. Between cars and really just too fast and bolting, and quicker now and gone between the opposite blocks but even this makes sense, or it could do. She is fast in the direction of the district where the ghost of the ghost of the ghost does live, with the one who is the lazy child – but also – also – also is – what? The ghost of the ghost of the ghost of the ghost, who is quick and odd and indistinct, but possibly – could she? – be the one? To have breathed this chaos of storm through the soup?

But it cannot be her. There is no reason for her. She is the ghost of the ghost of the ghost of the ghost and truly so like the ghost herself now that she is almost absolutely unbearable too. There is no reason for her to have come, and breathed here, and disappeared again, so just stop.

Portrait #15
Portfolio

In this portrait, the Palace is the subject and not just the background, like it always had been before. It was bulked and silent and grey-forgotten. The almost daughter knew that her mother had often gone there as a child, for her singing lessons, and it was where her brother met Yevgeniy on his way to school, and she did too if she walked with him, though in fact she had not for possibly weeks now. On the steps and railings up to it was where some people scraped tricks on their skateboards. But there were many alternative, better places for this. It was a sullen building, and always closed. Some of the long windows were sealed with planks and the ones that were not were barred-over glass. Even if a person had wanted to get inside – for any kind of reason at all – how this was supposed to occur was unclear. The expressions on the giant faces of the figures in short neckties cut into metal on the back wall were as once-triumphant and now worn-in as the ones on the statue at the centre of the machines.

Hello? Hello? Planet Earth here, said Valya. Or are you in a trance, or what?

The almost daughter blinked back from the chain that was stubborn on the doors at the top of the steps. Her limbs were still attached to the poles of what Valya called the ellipsis machine. It was like the bicycle with no wheels except the arms moved like skiing.

What? she said. Sorry. I just like this one.

Chains and padlocks on every one of the doors, and the windows blocked and plugged-endless ellipsis. She had opened her mouth in the bathroom three times to ask her brother about the leaflet in the cupboard bin, and three times she had left it to hang and then close.

When they sat in the middle by the statues at the end, there was a different view of the windows and doors, but there was also Valya explaining something. She said that she had heard about the thing from her cousin, and she spoke slowly and waited between her words.

Basically, she said. It's a pre-shoot you can do, to make a portfolio to take to the casting. It's professional, my cousin said.

When Elda looked to the almost daughter, it was as if to get the question to release from her instead. The almost daughter counted to ten and then eleven.

How much is it? Elda said at last. If it's professional like that, it won't be cheap.

Valya was even more lethargic in her answer. That says a lot already, she said. You realise?

Elda twitched something in the skin near her mouth.

You're asking first about the cost before you ask what it's like, or who it's with, said Valya. Don't you think that tells us something?

A portfolio would give us a kind of edge, said the almost daughter.

Valya turned. Well exactly, she said. Not everyone is going to have a proper portfolio. They're going to turn up with fuzzy printouts done by their mothers with their sofas behind them.

Elda was nodding. Definitely, she said. I sort of wasn't thinking about that. But it's obvious. It's great. We should definitely go.

I mean, I still need to get the details from my cousin, said Valya. It could still be a scam or whatever.

She stopped and aimed a final dramatic pause between Elda and the almost daughter.

Oh, she said. And I should probably mention that she said there might be only two spaces available.

She stood and stretched the other arm.

I'll have to let you know, she said.

They watched a video on perfectly smoked-looking eyelids, and then they watched two boys who were not on the screen but were grunting in real life on the heavier hitched-weight machines. The almost daughter said that she could see that one of the boys had an erection through his jeans. She could not actually see this at all, but it was good: Valya suggested going over to speak to them. Then, having risen, she sat down again. We'll be in a different league soon enough, she said.

The other thing the almost daughter had seen, and this was certain, was around the corner of the Palace building that the metalwork also bent around. There were more sharp-cut children in their neckties and badges, and they were marching or were zombies resurrected. One of the children around the corner was a girl who had two carved straight plaits, and another very straight carving sliced her body oddly. It was a rectangular carving that reached to the ground. It was a door and a door without a chain or a padlock.

Portrait #16
Tangle path

This is the portrait of metal blues and metal greens, and a bronze kind of colour that also hints dark scarlet. This is the portrait of tiny falling, and picking up again, and placing and finding the exact, right place. Sometimes there are lines of the same metal blue or of same bronze-maroon and now more amber, and sometimes the lines grow into two and much more. They always grow. They veer off and they tangle. They are branches and they are *This must be right*, and they knot and they are *No this must be right*. They are when and where and attempts, small, at why.

Songs and frantic is what they almost are, in mosaic.

This is the portrait of nearly microscopic metal on fingers, and the imprints left on finger skin, which are also maybe part of the portrait. And What the fuck are you doing? from a brother coming back, and this a good question by any measure, really.

68

This is a portrait of still trying to figure out, or at least figuring out whether to try to figure out. There is nothing decided but there is aching to decide. There is some kind of branch path to take. No – to make. This is the same portrait over several waking nights.

Portrait #17
The woman with the cave inside her

This is not a day in soup for the woman with the cave inside her. This is one of the other day types that come and these are the drop days with the blanks.

The drop that the woman with the cave inside her plummets into in this portrait, pleading, is the long ghost room after long ghost walking. The walking back is after dragging and digging: the digging is for posts of fence in mean ground, and the dragging is numbing wood in logs. All of the shovelling and walking is useless, and the holes are never deep enough in the mean ground, and feet are still fixed hard in frozen cloth not yet unwrapped in the long ghost room, and she knows that she must unwrap but she cannot. The feet of the ghost. The rawed hands of the ghost. She must unwrap and peel the ghost feet from the cloth before they are as dead as how dead her ached eyes are. They will decay and blacken more if she does not unpeel. The day for her turn to dry boots is when? It never comes and it never, ever comes and she is on the bunk until the next bell and still she is mean and numbed herself and decay-wrapped. The ghost. This ghost – just to touch this ghost.

Then the slump to utter blank. It is a void that now has no pain or needing but it really has no feeling at all. It is just as unbearable, but here it is, and so the woman with the cave inside her must bear it.

After the blank. Who? Someone now. Not in the ghost room of fear and bunks but in this room, of just one bed and one fear and the carpet scratches and the balcony door. And a some-one in the room, sudden on the carpet. There must have been the key-click, disguised, or it was blanked: it must have been. The woman with the cave inside her is here with someone by this window. Avoid the someone's face. Important to.

Just because she can't come today, says this someone on the carpet threads. She asked me to bring over your stuff and so I did.

Here, says the someone. And I have to take the old one.

You know they're essentially rotting, she says.

I'm just here because my mother can't, she says again, or has she said this already at all or not? The woman with the cave inside her is maybe the one repeating in her mind. It does happen.

Blank. Immense and blank.

Then out of blank and she is the one who is speaking: the woman with the cave inside her. It's alright, she says. It will be alright.

Her hand is dropped to the ghost room, unwrapping, and she is the one repeating and repeating. It's going to be alright, she says.

Blank.

I've just been thinking about all these things, says the some-one. I might just do it to see. I'll go and see. But also I keep on telling myself that and it just goes on and I keep going back.

There is none of the furniture in this room that there should be. The furniture even usually is not much, but now it is blanked away completely. There is only the balcony door and this someone.

And then I kind of thought, says the someone in this room who is not the atrocious ghost, for sure, but is the ghost of the ghost of the ghost of the ghost. Didn't you, she says. Weren't you. You know.

It was indeed the ghost of the ghost of the ghost of the ghost, then, who came before and clicked the key and ran. Now she is here again. She is speaking with her eyes to the carpet.

You and, she says. You know. You and. And I sort of think. I don't really have anyone to ask. What do you.

There is something that the woman with the cave inside could show her. There are the things she could say to her. Cave-hurt things.

I'm not really good at choosing, says the ghost of the ghost of the ghost of the ghost. I never know what's right to do. I stay away from having to choose. And people say we should leave it. My parents do. And maybe I just want to leave it too and it doesn't matter and I might get selected for— I might get picked and then everything changes. Or even if I don't, it's the thing I can do that makes me not so weird, somehow.

More now that the woman with the cave inside her does not understand at all – motorcycles, shoots? Shooting and fame and a shined life and travel. Or anyway just a way to be more normal.

Like I'm almost in a lift, you know, says the someone. Like I don't know where to get out or what to press. The lift in our building or the one here in yours and there are buttons that are safe and some not. If that makes sense.

It does make sense, to the woman with the cave inside. It makes sense for the duration of the moment it takes for the blankness to sink her white again.

Blank.

You can't let them stay wet, says the woman with the cave inside her to the atrocious ghost. She wants to say. She wants to touch. Her hand is gentle on bleeding skin.

Blank.

I really just came to bring you this stuff, says the someone on the carpet and shrugging. That's all. Just my mother couldn't come and so I'm here instead.

Or: Can I look behind the mirror hook, maybe?

Don't forget to wash the cabbages properly, she says.

Portrait #18
Materials

In the evening and dark, the machines in the broken oval behind the Palace looked different. The bandaged rings and bars and wheels and pulleys and other components had been vehicles, or weapons, and now they looked violent. The almost daughter could not believe that she had touched them and grasped at them, but it was a different version that had done this, after all. She walked past them and up the slab steps and turned, and then was inside the small carved door that was not quite invisible now, when propped open.

It was like the station that was enormous and had been built but never used, because of something to do with gauges or widths. There were parties there, at the station hall, or at least there was drinking there, and there clearly had been here too, in the Palace: there were cans and there were floor marks from dead fires. There were painted wall children in this entrance section like the carved ones on the outer wall. At their feet were the crushed cans and flat cigarettes.

It is here, said a woman who was not painted. If you've come along for the vote.

The almost daughter followed her into the room she was pointing to, down steps and underneath a bracket for a flag.

The man who was standing on the stage-ledge at the front was the man with the broken briefcase. Of course he was. Behind him, there were more painted people, and they were children not in uniform and women with baskets of rolls of baked bread. The flakes that had splintered from the bread were like real crusts.

The man with the broken briefcase said the same things about the monument collapsed in the river, except that he was using different, more fierce words. Instead of Disgrace, he said. Absolute shame. Instead of Scandal, he swore.

At certain moments it was necessary to hold down the switch inside the almost daughter's skull that kept her from recognising people on the seats. There was a woman who could have been the woman who had spat at the portrait in the lift, on the fifth floor, and she was next to another woman and her son who looked a lot like the mother and her deaf adult son who lived on the tenth or eleventh floor. There was a man who, if the anti-recognition button had not been in effect, could have been a colleague of her father's at the gas plant.

On the stage-ledge, the man with the broken briefcase was now talking not exactly about the monument. He was speaking with the words Danger, and Possible.

We clearly can't ignore the fact that we are likely to come up against some strong opposition, he said. There are people who will find what we are doing unpatriotic, or treacherous or just not needed, he said. He said that this was had happened in other towns.

The woman who was the woman from the fifth floor called out. It was her because she looked like she could easily spit again.

We're ready for it, she said. I am, at least.

Other people shouted out about truth and responsibility.

It's just something we do have to be aware of, said the man.

There was arguing that was a kind of arguing that was more about what other people might say and do, rather than what the people who were there were thinking. It was the empty folded-straight seats that were arguing and were louder and then there was a vote, and the almost daughter was certainly still not properly listening. She was examining the grates along the tops of the walls. They must be what turned into the strips that looked like gutters on the outside of the Palace.

Those in favour of simply restoring the monument, said the man with the broken briefcase on the ledge.

The almost daughter did not count hands.

And those in favour of an actual museum, said the man.

There were hands again, and again, the almost daughter did not count. When her brain seemed to think that it did want to count, she let it count the rolls of bread in the baskets that hung on the arms of the pride-faced mural women. They were doing something good for other people. They were feeding the children in their ties and uniforms and the statue athletes outside and all the country, really. It was a bright and painted and solid story.

And then there were the crusts of bread flaking away that were holes in the bright story: sinkholes that tugged. But if the story did have murked parts, they were part of the picture.

76

Are you voting or just stretching? said a woman behind her. You need to be clear or honestly, what's the point.

The almost daughter stretched further and up and it was purely because it was good for her posture. Valya had said this was important twice a day. It was something about the spine and it was crucial. Or more than twice, was what Valya had said. In a queue or waiting for the trolley bus or at any spare moment, so this was why, purely. One arm straight up towards the ceiling cracks and wall grates. Her ribs were opening up and this was all.

An excited and very loud man was saying that of course the museum was the essential step. It's right, he said. It's not enough to have a stone in the river that no one ever sees. It's right.

The problem with the stretching was that a neck lengthened upwards could help a person to see to the front rows, and that the switch that stopped recognition had failed fully now. It did not work on people with half-purpled hair. Oksana was sitting close – very close – to a boy the almost daughter remembered from the meeting at the school and from her brother's year. He had a ring midway up one of his ears that he never had at school, or she had never seen it. She never would have looked at him. When her brother spoke about him with his friends, they mimicked him in a high, nasal pitch. But Oksana's shoulder was pressed to his. It was.

It will take time and even more in energy, the man with the broken briefcase said. We are going to have to remember that.

And not forget the risks, said a woman.

And for another thing, we need more materials, said the man. We need more. We need everything you have.

77

From the broken briefcase he took the stack of photographs and papers and what looked like they might be diaries, and there were more now already than there had been at the school.

Photographs, letters, whatever you have, he said. We need the truth and all the stories we've lost. We need them back.

The almost daughter stretched upwards again, though certainly not towards letters and photographs.

There was only what happened on the way out that was complicated, after the arguing over what had been argued already. The man had clasped his broken briefcase together and said that it was getting late. Finally, people were standing and the seats were springing up in relief, and the relief was the almost daughter's as well.

This was when Oksana and the boy with the feather ring in his ear were near her. They were still so close to each other. They were out of the carved door now and leaving too, and close.

Hey, said Oksana. I thought you might come.

The boy with the ring midway up his ear said something about having lost the bet. The almost daughter began to ready something to say about checking for somewhere for shelter if there was a day when it rained, but as it formed she knew it could only make sense if she also spoke about the training. The training would have to come with the casting and the modelling, and it really did not make sense at all to say any of this to someone who could sit upside down on the chair by the director's office, and who screamed at teachers and was just who she was. The versions of the almost daughter were in knots.

Did you find your gloves in there? said Oksana. Or your hat this time?

The almost daughter's knotting was becoming something different, maybe, but things were too fast to find what it was.

Good to keep an eye out, said Oksana, and she was winking or she was possibly just blinking this time. You never know where what you're looking for might just turn up, she said.

The almost daughter needed to say something – anything – and tripped hideously on one of the slab steps, and did not. Oksana and the boy left together, still close.

Portrait #19
Portraits in colour

Blue and blue and green and black. And a poem read some-where? What was that? Something about a monument built – where? And this was all in her head as she walked and not even with the real beads yet, so she was mad.

Portrait #20
Portraits in ice

This is a portrait out of order. It is out of sequence but not out of place.

It is the portrait, mainly, of the sculptures of ice that the almost daughter visited one winter in the car park that was outside the closed theatre. She was eight or nine or ten years old and she was the height of the deer that did not have antlers, being pared into shape beside the deer that did. The antlers were taller than she was and gleaming. Everything looked wet and glittered. The unfinished giant peacock was taller than her and the completed standing man on a long boat was taller. The church with its turrets still not rounded was taller than absolutely everyone, and the ladders up to it were double extended.

The woman who was holding her hand, through her glove, was the height of the ugly mermaid on the rock. The mermaid had awful, enormous carved lips, but the woman's face was hard to see. She looked down or at the sculptures or at the many tools for cutting and did not look straight at the almost daughter.

She did speak. It was the woman holding her hand who had explained that the sculptures were still being hacked from cube blocks, and that this was why so many still had extra corners and were halfway, only, to being what they would be. They were not final and exact, as they had been in the other years when the almost daughter had come with her parents. The woman said that this day was the right day to come because the sculptors and artists had just nine hours to turn a plain and measured six-sided block into something that was named and beautiful. The almost daughter did not say that the mermaid was never going to be beautiful.

You can see the process this way, said the woman. You can see where things come from. It's better to know.

The woman had been saying this from the start, and she had bought the almost daughter both soft chestnuts and a milk ice cream on a stick, when her father would have made her choose, if he had let her have either at all. But then the woman was saying it again, and too much.

You have to see what happened before, she said.

They were standing beneath the crystal-like church and the ladders and the ice priest beside it, who was nearly complete except for his eyes. There was a ladder up to his neck as well. He was really much too big for the church.

You have to know, said the woman. You have to. I want you to see— I need to give you—

The almost daughter let the woman's hand loose from hers to crumple the chestnut-greased paper into her pocket, but also because the woman's voice was too strange.

82

Then the woman was on the car park ground in the blades of ice that had been chipped from the church.

I think you should get up, said the almost daughter. She could feel that people were beginning to look.

The woman jerked her head – finally – directly up to the almost daughter. Her eyeballs were horrified, or scared.

You can't, she said. Not you. You can't be.

The almost daughter only wanted her to be quiet. She wanted her to freeze still like the sculptures.

You're gone, said the woman, not loudly, but distinctly. Because of me you're lost. You can't be here.

The opposite of freezing and stopping was what the woman did. She kicked her feet in their boots at the ice blades, and she stood half up, fell, and was up again. She moved her kicking to the priest's sharp white robe and now she was hissing and now she was loud.

No, said the almost daughter, which was pointless.

The woman's boot cracked a fold from the robe of the priest, and she looked surprised and maybe thrilled for a moment, but then she shook her head away. She scanned with her eyes and nodded when she was facing towards the only sculpture that was larger than the church and its priest. It was a kind of wall that was made of men and women who were holding long axes and saws above their heads. A machine that also seemed to be for cutting formed part of the wall as well, and the shoulders of the men and women were square. When they had passed this section of the sculptures before, the woman holding the almost daughter's hand had not wanted to stop at all, even though the almost daughter had wanted to ask her if the shoulders were supposed to be so square, or if they had just not been properly shaped yet.

83

The woman was back at the wall of the workers now and her boot foot was kicking at their boot feet. The pieces that were coming off were bigger than what she had crunched from the priest's robe. The largest chunk that severed away, before a real man with a real chisel pulled the woman down, was a piece that was the size of a head. It looked like one of the workers' heads: it could have been. It wasn't like this, the woman was hissing.

The almost daughter did not entirely remember the rest. The woman was down and staying down, and people were still shouting at and around her. Someone must have asked the almost daughter something, and she must have given them an answer, because then they were telephoning her mother at home, and her mother arrived and so did her father. It was her father who took her back to the apartment, and her mother who towed the woman up from the car park ground and went with her and looked so silent. The head-boot was blank and cracked and left behind.

Afterwards, the almost daughter's father and mother had been talking in their room. Her father had been sleeping there again but the almost daughter still liked to check. That night he was saying: But maybe they need to know, and her mother was saying: I can't. We can't. I can't. We can't. She said: And it's the last time she takes her out alone.

It was, as far as the almost daughter could remember. This is the portrait of how it is that questions form, and freeze in place, or puddle back to formless water.

But now: You can read her letters, the woman had hissed. Her rawed hands and scream-pain and names, she had spat. And she's lost and lost and I lost her, she had whispered.

84

Portrait #21
In questions

This is the portrait of the two newest questions that would not leak away and dissolve. They were attached to the almost daughter now and weighed at her, and were invisible to each other, or more than that: they avoided each other and were anti-magnetic. They ducked into shadows when the other one was close.

The first question appeared to come from Valya, though of course it did not only come from her. It came through her, and through her smirks. It came, and it had always been coming, as she slowed on the ellipsis machine. Elda had already gone home.

I mean, seriously, Valya said. It's like she just doesn't care sometimes.

The almost daughter signalled agreement. She left early last time too, she said.

Whatever, said Valya. It's just – well, it's a shame.

Because Valya so clearly wanted her to, the almost daughter asked. What's a shame? she said.

The thing is, said Valya. Come down for a second. At least it makes my decision here easier.

Again, she wanted to be asked. What decision? said the almost daughter.

Valya leaned against the frame behind her. She said that this was something strictly between only the two of them, of course. That they had to be honest about what hope in hell they had if they were just wasting time on the prehistoric junk outside the Palace, and watching videos. That there was still the matter of the pre-shoot portfolio that her cousin mentioned and that might change the game.

I was kind of wondering, said the almost daughter.

And I did more than kind of wonder, said Valya. Someone had to, eventually. Like I said before, though, the spaces are limited.

The almost daughter was motionless externally, and inside she pictured something falling into place, like the weights slotting back into their brackets with a click.

Only two left, like I thought, said Valya. But it's fine because I've made my decision. I won't say it was completely easy but I'm pretty happy with it now, I think. If you are.

Valya spoke more and made only the click sound. She was talking about the portfolio, and the click came, and the date and how to get there, and – click-lock.

Sounds good, said the almost daughter. All sounds good.

Just probably best not to tell Elda, said Valya. Anyway, you can take a few days to think.

And so a question like: Are you genuinely dedicated? Something like: Are you normal and here? Something like this and also like: Do you or do you not want this chance to have this power and have this secret? But mostly like: Are you normal? Can you prove it?

The second question was already half there, as the back-stitching of the first, front question. The second question became the front question in one of the corridors in the basement at the school.

The almost daughter knew where the lockers for new students were. She knew that they were in the basement. It was where the boy from a military school had had his locker for five weeks one year, before he was found to be storing knives there, and was sent back to the military school or somewhere worse. All of the new students' lockers were there. But there were never many new or even once-new students and the basement was always empty by the time she could arrive. She had to wait for anyone who might care if they saw her to have gone before she could go the basement.

Two days after the first question, though, it was not empty. It was empty initially, and she was just about to leave, and then it was not empty and someone was there.

Oksana came towards her along the corridor in a way that seemed to last eternally.

Just getting my sneaky scarf, she said. Weird how you can end up leaving things like that.

The almost daughter watched Oksana bend and open the locker with a sticker of a skull on it. It had been partly peeled but was certainly a skull, with hollow eyeholes on a shield. Oksana brought something out of the locker that in every way was not a scarf. It was another leaflet from another stack.

You didn't take this one, that other night, she said. Even though you voted and I saw you.

The skull could have belonged to the military school boy, or it could have come from Oksana. The question was growing and coming from Oksana.

I'm still deciding, said the almost daughter.

Well, fuck that, said Oksana. You'll need to be quick. We're starting the weekend after next. Read it.

The almost daughter looked at the paper and saw disjointed letters. Starting what? she said.

There are places we need to get to up the river for research and also the cemetery, said Oksana. We're camping. Not like there are any hotels.

The almost daughter bit into her cheek, and this was like a knife or a shield. A cemetery was – a knife, or a shield?

As in, you're camping, with us, said Oksana.

The almost daughter's back teeth bit firmer.

You don't need a tent if that's the problem, said Oksana. Lavrentiy has two. All the rest is on the sheet.

There was a split between wondering how many people in which permutations could fit in two tents, and the biting of cheeks that might halt the numbers. The words on the paper were still cluttered code. Lavrentiy was the boy with the feather earring and the almost daughter knew she had known this.

I said I'm still deciding, she said.

Whatever, said Oksana. Bring thick socks. And something for the mosquitoes on the river.

She packed a clump of the leaflets into her bag and crashed the locker door four times until it shut.

Then she was up and already smaller, down the corridor.

88

It was Lavrentiy who said I'd find you here, she said. He said he's seen you come down here most days after lessons, like you've been waiting for something.

There was the beige part of the wall behind her and then there was the green and where they met. There was Oksana and then there was not listening to anything Oksana said.

Of course, maybe it's just another coincidence, she said.

Portrait #22
Portrait in screens

Between and through the questions, there was still television. The programme that the almost daughter's mother liked to watch was the programme about competing and cooking. There were countdown alarms and challenges and disasters and one woman's oven gloves caught fire. Someone was always sent home at the end and the almost daughter's mother always shook her head. On one night, the almost daughter asked her what she watched the programme for. Her mother looked confused and said: I watch it every day.

On another night, there was the programme that was competing again, but with singing and dancing. At the beginning there were the small girls and one boy who sang old songs with old instruments playing. The girls wore their red and gold dresses and headpieces and this part at the start was not for competing, and was maybe about

90

traditions or history. When the older girls and women came they wore make-up, and sang newer songs that were sometimes in English. It was competing and probably one or some of them would get rich if they won or nearly won, or some of them would be escorts and whores. Some of them, maybe, or even just one, were only doing it because their friends were as well, and if they had the chance to do it and then decided not to do it, they would be unnatural and messed-up.

Stop getting ideas, said the almost daughter's brother, who pretended he did not like this programme but watched the older girls and commented on them. He especially commented if they tripped as they walked or had voices when they sang that he said were like a man's.

On a different night, they watched the news, while also watching their phones and eating soup. There was something again about the orphanages, and the almost daughter had seen this before. Children were being taken and adopted in other countries, and it was somehow connected to people now no longer going to church enough. The almost daughter's brother said that he had heard about one boy who was eight and was taken away by two men from France, and that the men had done disgusting things to the boy.

Her mother said that it couldn't be true, and her brother said that it was definitely true. He pointed with his jaw to the screen when it showed two men who had bags across their shoulders and were being shown around an orphanage. The scene changed to night-time and they were back in the dormitory and choosing between a row of children in bunkbeds, and then there was a car that was speeding away.

They're actors, said the almost daughter's father. You know it's not an actual recording.

It's a reconstruction, said the almost daughter's brother, and there were letters on the screen that said Reconstruction. That means it did happen and really, he said.

The section of the news that was longest was about preparations for the parades in other cities. They were the military parades and were still six weeks away, but they were important because of the anniversary and because of this the preparations had started to be shown on both the short news and the long news. The images showed tanks and very old men in medals, and very young men practising marching in the squares.

They're having something here as well, this year, said the almost daughter's brother. Or maybe not a parade but a kind of rally.

The almost daughter's father on the sofa nodded. Someone told me that, too, he said.

But this is the thing, said the almost daughter's brother. There's also some mental activist group that's planning a way to attack the parades.

Attack them? said the almost daughter, and her mother looked across the table to her. Her brother was watching her father's face.

There is some kind of group, said her mother. Dasha at the bank was saying. She said they're coming to the schools as well.

She was looking across to the almost daughter and waiting for something. Did they come to yours? she said.

What kind of group? said the almost daughter's father.

To attack the parades and rallies, said her brother, slowly, with his chin pushed to show that this was obvious. And to mess with stuff in general and say everything is lies.

So they came to the school? said the almost daughter's mother.

No one really cares, said her brother. Nobody went and nobody cares.

Did you know as well? her mother said and she was looking across the table, still.

The almost daughter said she'd had no idea. The news changed to news about the borders again. She checked her phone and a message from Valya said: You'd better be deciding. Tick tock tick tock. Then there was the yellow face with one bulged eye.

Beads in place and tucking, curved, and leading.

Portrait #23
Portrait in answers

This is the portrait of one Yes, in the stairwell. The stairwell was Valya's and Valya had said that Elda's poses looked like children's poses pretending to be models' poses. She said the same thing, or had started to, about the almost daughter's poses, and then the almost daughter had done something with her lips that they had just seen in one of the videos. Valya had said that it was actually okay. Elda had not left early, but had not stayed when the almost daughter said she would.

Good, said Valya when the Yes had surfaced. Let's do this fucking thing properly, finally.

She said that she would make the arrangements.

This is the portrait of the second Yes, back in the basement corridor, near the locker where the knives had been, and where Oksana was waiting for the almost daughter instead of the almost daughter waiting. There was something flashing and brilliant about this fact alone.

Good, Oksana said to this Yes. I knew you would. I just knew. And we need you.

She said more about insect repellent spray, and the monument and the museum, and passing paper in the hallways to keep things secret. She had said: Good, most importantly, and she had said: We need you, and the almost daughter had said: Okay.

Portrait #24
The woman with the cave inside her

This is the portrait of one more way.

The woman with the cave inside her is standing and holding what she has been given: she is holding what she has been given and it is cold air. Or she is holding it and it is making the air cold. She has been given a milk ice cream on a stick and cloaked in chocolate and now the ghost of the ghost of the ghost of the ghost is still in the middle of the room and sometimes saying things. This ghost of the ghost of the ghost of the ghost brought the ice cream, in the bag with vegetables and papers. The woman with the cave inside her is holding the ice cream by the stick that she can feel and is cold through the wrapper. Children she sees from the window eat these. They drop them and they cry or once she saw one who licked the melted wreck from the concrete.

The ghost of the ghost of the ghost of the ghost has said that she has agreed to something. She has said this now so many times that the woman with the cave inside her is not sure if the ghost of the ghost of the ghost of the ghost has agreed to one thing or more than one. She has agreed to the thing she says is shoots or shooting, and she has agreed to this mostly to keep herself not monstrous. She says monstrous and abnormal and just not right.

And then the museum stuff, she says. But only really doing it just for now. Not signing anything and I won't do all of it. And there are obviously some things I just won't do.

The ice cream is definitely slicking in the foil. The woman with the cave inside should be opening the foil – but then she would have to be eating the ice cream. She does not know if biting is needed, and this would be difficult, with the cold especially, or sucking which is or could also be disaster. She has bought these things before, once or twice or maybe more, but they were not for herself to have.

Because, says the ghost of the ghost of the ghost of the atrocious ghost. Because I'm not really wanting to attack anything but I just think it's maybe right.

She is not pacing now but sitting with crossed legs on the floorboards.

And a tiny bit because of the people there, she says. They're different but not really in a bad way.

The woman with the cave holds the ice cream and waits.

They're brave, says the ghost of the ghost of the ghost of the ghost. Like they don't care what anyone thinks. Especially—

Well, all of them, she says.

She says something else and then something else.

And you know that time with the sculptures and you let me have chestnuts and also one of those, says the ghost of the ghost of the ghost of the ghost. And you said we had to know or I had to know where things came from and what they were before.

The woman with the cave inside her moves closer and is holding out the cold in the foil. The ghost of the ghost of the ghost of the ghost takes it and tears open the wrapper and looks in.

You were right, says the ghost of the ghost of the ghost of the atrocious ghost. So it's also for you and for all that.

She stands and tips the contents inside the wet foil into a bowl that is only slightly crusted. The stick separates and she lifts it and licks it. She takes a spoon from the sink that is not crusted at all because she washed it herself before the pacing and talking.

She hands the bowl and the spoon and the ice cream back to the woman with the cave inside her. It is a solution that is perfect and effective: this method does not require bites or sucking. And she did know. Of course she recognised the wrapper type. She can feel-remember a small hand in a glove and yes, it was the last time. It must have been. There were all the things that had come from cubes and yes, she had wanted to show the becoming. She had wanted to show what it was be brave and not care what anyone else was thinking too—

The letters and the photograph. Behind the mirror? Probably. Quite probably.

So that's why too, says the ghost of the ghost of the ghost of the one who became the ghost. It's mixed up together but it's part of it. It's a part of it that's big, if you want to know. I'm not good at explaining but I needed to tell you.

This is the portrait of one more way to say Yes.

Part III

Portrait #25
Faces, portfolio

The portfolio shoot was in the shopping centre in the part of the town by the seven-layer car park. It was where, in the central section on the ground floor, the almost daughter's father had used to bring her to meet a blue woman in a crown who was a snow queen and have a photograph taken with her. She had had to make a smiling face for the photographs, even though the blue woman's dress smelled of plastic and the crown had a pearl that was missing from it and left a hollow like a cracked eye socket. She had had to make the same happy face every year, and now she was practising the final faces that Valya had decided were best in the glass of one of the shop-fronts on the top floor. They were the final faces before they would go down to join the queue at the marquees below. It was Saturday, and they had told Elda not to go to school, and to meet them at the park with the empty fountains, later. This was one of the versions of herself now.

Powerful, said Valya. Do that one again.

The almost daughter deepened her eyebrows.

I mean, fine, said Valya. Now seductive.

The almost daughter tensed the frown further and bit her lips together from inside her mouth.

I don't know, said Valya. I think it's more like this.

She made the face that had been the face that she had called the commanding face, and was also the same as the wild innocence face. The almost daughter replicated her jaw, and Valya said that this was better, and then it was time to join the queue of the girls who were taller and whose hair was larger and fresher. When they asked which modelling academy it was that the almost daughter and Valya went to, Valya said it was in a different town.

Inside the marquee, there was no false queen, no silver pine tree with its branches spread like arms, and no glittered line of baubles with bronze cursive lettering. Where the bulky and golden painted throne had been, in front of a cartoon landscape of a forest, there was a plain white canvas screen held up vertically that also curved and became the floor. The camera was possibly the same, on three legs, though probably it was not the same. The white screen was not completely plain where a wipe mark looked like lipstick on it.

If you have outfits you can change over there, said the man who was next to the man at the camera. He pointed to a sheet loose over two chairs that was close to the men at the back of the marquee. The chairs were as tall as where the almost daughter's ribs would be. She said that she had left her outfits in the car, and the man next to the man at the camera said that there must be a lot of cars outside somewhere with outfits and paperwork and prizes in them.

And mothers who somehow forgot to check that their daughters had everything before they drove off, he said.

The man at the camera told the almost daughter that what she had paid for was sixteen photos, and that he could give advice if it was needed, but within a reasonable limit, of course, because the price was for the portfolio itself and not full professional curatorial services. Then he said that he was ready.

The almost daughter made her face be the innocent face first, and then she made seductive, and powerful, and cruel, and her ankles were stiff in the shoes she had borrowed from Valya that were tight and too high. She crossed her legs and never stood quite with her hips straight to the man at the camera. Valya was through two layers in the adjacent marquee, and was maybe joking with her man at the camera, who was maybe saying that her faces were stunning. He was asking her how it was possible that she wasn't signed with a school already or even an agency or an advertising firm. And still, all of this was fine, because the almost daughter was here and had not been stopped in the queue and told to go home. She had not been told that there was some mistake: she had not been laughed at more than anyone else. And while Elda was in bed or helping her mother, the almost daughter had something that connected her to Valya, and would make her be less freakish, and better.

Two of the men at the end of the marquee were talking and nodding and leaning forward. The almost daughter was still doing faces and angles. The one without sunglasses was looking at her, and the one with sunglasses was looking, clearly, too. The almost daughter knew without hearing what they were saying. They were saying that it honestly blew their minds that girls like this would come here at all. I don't know why they bother, they were saying. The average ones – the clueless ones – I can understand, but when one of these comes in it's frankly insulting, they were saying to each other. You can tell straight away, they said. There's something not right. Is she even a girl? said the sunglasses. Do we need to start getting them to prove it, to be sure?

The man at the camera, and the man next to him, nodded with the man from the back, and they were going to ask her to leave and not return. They were going to ask her to pay double the price for the portfolio and for wasting their time.

He says what about those buttons, said the man at the camera. What about unbuttoning just a bit, from the top.

The almost daughter was stuck in her face. The man from the back without sunglasses who had not told her to take her backpack and leave was pointing to his chest in his leather jacket.

Tell her it's the melancholy, he said. It's in her eyes and her jawline. It just works.

The man next to the man at the camera said: He's not supposed to speak to you directly. He's not even really here, is the thing.

Tell her the melancholy works, and we just need to see a little more of where it's from, said the man in the leather jacket from the back. More of the vulnerability, he said.

The man next to the man at the camera pointed at the top of his black shirt. The black shirt was already unbuttoned to hair and a cross that was silver on thin chain.

The almost daughter unbuttoned from the collar of the shirt that was the fourth she had tried in the mirror in the bathroom before she had gone to meet Valya. She unbuttoned to where chest hair and a cross would be, and then, she unbuttoned one more.

104

That's it, said the man who had come from the back. Tell her that's better, and now the sad eyes again.

The almost daughter made the heartbroken and pleading face, which was not one she had practised on the upper floor. On the bus, Valya had already said it had made her look too desperate and weird. She did this face and others and the camera ticked.

She did the faces and the man who had stood up and spoken walked to the back of the marquee again. He reached the chairs and picked up his coffee cup and drank, and wiped his lips with the back of his hand and the hairs on it like the chest in the shirt. He put down the cup, and lifted one small card from the table and now was coming back to the camera.

You can give her this, he said to the man at the camera. You can tell her we might have something for her, depending on what she's prepared to do.

The man at the camera took the card and brought it to the almost daughter. The back of his hand was pale and bald.

Tell her it's the kind of madness with the melancholy, said the man with the leather jacket and haired hands. It's unusual. We could find something for her.

The almost daughter's hand moved to button her shirt, and then decided to leave it as it was.

And we can repay the cost of the portfolio, if she calls, said another man with sunglasses at the back of the marquee. He picked up his phone and bent towards it and yawned.

Outside the marquees, on the benches near the queue, one girl was crying loudly into her hands, and one was crying silently, pretending not to. Valya was close to the silent girl, whose face was shaking but not moving in its features.

What took so long with you? said Valya. The girl who was loud was nearly choking.

The almost daughter looked at her watch. She had been in the marquee for twenty-eight minutes.

The camera stopped working, she said. Or something.

Valya had been waiting and therefore possibly had not been joking with the men with cameras and laptops in the left-hand marquee.

It was probably the seductive face that did it, said the almost daughter. I know it wasn't perfect but I didn't expect it to break the camera.

As they walked, Valya said that the camera not working was another thing that showed it wasn't such a professional service after all. She made a face she had not practised: a revolted but also disappointed face. She made the same face on the bus when the almost daughter asked, when it was nearly time to get off and meet Elda, if there were men at the back of the marquee she was in and if they had said something while she was there. Valya made the face and said that they probably were scouts from agencies and would only take one in a million girls, and at the same time all their agencies were probably fake or dirty anyway. They changed their shoes and cleaned off the make-up in the bus and left the wet tissue towels in clumps on the seat.

When she asked her brother in the bathroom if he thought she had a melancholy madness, he said she absolutely did. By absolutely, he said, I mean you fifty per cent do. He said he would leave it to her to guess which fifty per cent she had.

Portrait #26
The woman with the cave inside her

Sometimes she wakes into this. For no reason. Sometimes it is before sent letters and long low buildings and scream-names and perpetual drag and the damp and blisters. Sometimes she wakes to the before, like this.

Into what? Into this. Scratched desks and classroom. Someone's name and someone else's. A classroom, say, with paints laid out: a palette on each desk and stiff paper. Why does she remember this? A palette of hard blocks of colour, and the boy next to her just because of his surname, who does not wash the brush enough before he takes a different colour. He grimes yellow into grey, and nice green into grey, and white into slop of smeared browns and grey. Can't you wash it first? she says. He shrugs because he does not care about colours. He needs mathematics and physics and divisions and he will maybe go to the school sometime soon that is special for mathematics and science. Will there be colour there, in palettes? She thinks not. She does not think there would be.

She paints what they are meant to paint, first. She paints seven women strong in a field and the harvest is good and the grain is good, even though her mother has said that often the grain, from the fields, is not good. In the city they do not see the grain but they wait in queues whole afternoons and they chew the bread that tastes of wool. But her mother says this is not the worst, of course. She paints the golds and browns of the field, except that they are grey-gold, grey-brown.

She paints the field and the teacher says it is sufficient, and then it is time to be free with the paint, just for a freedom of twenty minutes. The boy paints a field again and she could too, or she should, because even with the free twenty minutes, she can show what her mind is committed to, even when she is free to choose. But she does not paint field. She paints only the women. And the boy beside her, who – yes, she remembers – once told her that her hair was angelic, and she blushed but she felt trapped in her face, and she no longer wanted to speak to him, and since then he has muttered things about her – he looks at her painting and now he mutters. Typical, he mutters. Creep weird, he mutters. He told others that she had not let him touch her hair and this was a creep and weird thing to do. He muttered then and mutters now.

He is not so bad. He could say these things louder, but he does not really care because of his hopes for the special institute. He only mutters, but it makes her realise. She flushes the women in her painting on stiff paper with brown and grey from the bristles. She blots them. Yes – blot the one who looks like the green-eye girl, most. Green eyes never say that her hair is angelic but they smile at her sometimes and this is

108

more than angels. What is it? Something very wrong. Make her grey in the painting now and melt her. Brown and grey and pasted away. The green-eye girl, who says the things that make the teachers grit into their teeth, who gives a room a voltage, a shock-charge.

Before and wasted – why should she think of this? Why she should paint all this now as she wakes. The girl with the green eyes and aching eyes barely ever spoke to her, but something was there then, even before. Before the – before – before – before. Inexplicable. Or is it? Or just a colour kept inside her. It is the fault of the ghost of the ghost of the ghost of the ghost, who came and spoke of mutters herself, and paintings, or was it photographs. The ghost of the ghost of the ghost of the ghost said: Creep. Yes, she said this, too.

If she could paint now. Bring her back. Bring green. Bring aching. Bring back and hold. But – how.

She gave a room and a mind a voltage, she says.

Portrait #27
Faces, bones

This is a long and many-threaded portrait. The plan for the expedition along the river, and for the tents with people close inside them, and for whatever was going to happen in the forest, was not a plan the almost daughter knew in detail. The plan that she – or this version of herself – did know was her own pre-plan. The pre-plan was for explaining and hiding. To Valya and Elda she had said she had to visit her aunt in her house outside the town. There was no toilet in her house and the one in the shed at the end of the garden had cobwebs and insects and only newsprint to wipe with, but the soil had to be turned after winter and the greenhouse needed to be covered in foil and the vegetables needed to be planted in rows. To her mother, the almost daughter said she would be staying with Elda's aunt and uncle, in the house they lived in outside the town in summer, with its shed and cobwebs and stiff printed sheets. The hard soil needed to be turned after the winter and the aunt and uncle needed help because Elda's mother could not help. The almost daughter's mother said it was good that she would have the fresh air and also that she should wash her hands and under her nails, especially after digging. She gave her soap to take in a paper box. Her brother said she would come back a peasant. Valya said the toilet would be hell on earth, but that the digging would maybe be good for lean muscle.

Where she was waiting for the van that was going to take her to nobody's aunt and nobody's uncle, and to not even a shed for a toilet, was next to the main road out of the town. There was a bridge overhead and it held six hanging lamps. It was where Oksana had told her to come when she had tapped on the almost daughter's shoulder in the hallway.

At eight o'clock, when Oksana had said the van would come, the cars that were passing in the lanes on the side that the almost daughter and her backpack were on were families who really were driving to uncles and aunts and some had shovels and buckets on their roofs. By nine o'clock, there were fewer of them. A car with blue rotating lights screamed past and the same car blared back again the other way. At ten, the almost daughter opened the carton of chocolates that her mother had packed for Elda's aunt.

At ten thirty-five, when a van pulled in and stopped tilted on the kerb where it was not supposed to stop, the almost daughter climbed in and did not see Oksana. The man who was driving was a man she did not know, with a circle in his chin that was a piercing or a pimple. Others in the van were from the meeting at the Palace of Creativity and Youth, and others were not from the meeting. There were two boys at the very back from the school and they raised their hands to her. The woman who had tugged open the slide door threw the almost daughter's backpack onto the pile that was next to the boys at the back, in a space that two seats had been pulled out of. The pile, of tents and sleeping bags and more than three enormous saws, shuddered and the van tipped back down to the road.

The almost daughter sat in the one remaining seat, next to a boy who had taken off his headphones. He asked if she wanted to smoke. She said no.

What about those? he said, and pointed. She was holding the package of chocolates for the aunt.

She passed the chocolates to the boy and he ate one, and then another and another, steadily, as the van clattered on. There was music and smoking and swapping of seats. The main road narrowed to smaller roads and tracks. The boy had his headphones back on as he ate, and drummed his fingers on his knees and on the headrest in front of him, and a girl with a bald head turned around and pounded him with a metal flask. There were short, strange names like Rabbit and Meatflea, and it meant that they all knew each other.

The almost daughter had beads in her eye-mind.

When woods had been passing the window for an hour, and the tracks were still tracks but were mostly holes, the van stopped and the music from the front also stopped. The woman by the sliding door who had opened it for the almost daughter before leaned forward and pulled it open again. Outside, there was a man in a khaki jacket and he helped the woman and then the others down, and made the pile of tents from the back of the van a new pile of tents on the ground below. Behind the man and the pile there were trees, and further on there were tents that were already standing and a small orange fire in the patch between them.

The boy beside the almost daughter was pushing her, not hard, on her shoulder. It's as far as we can go on four wheels, he said. He gave her the empty package from the chocolates. She stood and climbed down and held the khaki arm of the man outside the van.

She found her backpack in the pile, on top of one huge saw, and followed others who were moving to the fire. They were already unwrapping tents and poles. They were going to be putting up the tents. The almost daughter did not know how to put up a tent.

Hey, said a voice that was from behind her.

The almost daughter turned and was facing the boy with the feather earring from the school. He was Lavrentiy, unless he also had another strange short name in the woods.

There's space for you in ours already, he said. Oksana told you. She was meant to tell you.

Right, said the almost daughter. She did.

The almost daughter did not say to Lavrentiy that what Oksana had also said was that the van would come at eight o'clock and that she would be in the van as well.

I think there's space, at least, said Lavrentiy. He took the almost daughter's backpack from her. If you don't mind things kind of cosy, he said.

He led the almost daughter through to the tents already standing, and the fire. He smelled of smoke wisps and the faces around the fire were shadowed and then bright and flickered. The almost daughter checked again. None of the flickers was the face of Oksana.

Lavrentiy said that she should roll out her mat and then come to have a drink by the fire. The almost daughter did not have a mat. Her eyelids were dragging and the fire faces were laughing and definitely not one of them was Oksana. She was wearing the thick socks already and was cold. She told Lavrentiy that she thought she was tired.

If you're sure, he said. I can't stop you being wise.

He gestured to the fire one more time and said that she could always come later, if she wanted. He hugged his arms around her and this was unexpected and the almost daughter felt like planks but hugged back. He said that he would see her in the morning and that the front of the tent was better for bladder needs, but worse for the mosquitoes, if they were out yet.

The almost daughter lay in the sleeping bag, which had come from under her father's bed. She was perpendicular to the other laid-out bags, and this meant that feet would press into her later, or else be on top of her, but this also might be warmer. Outside the tent there was the laughing and guitar, and they might not ever come in to sleep anyway. They needed rest for the next day, Lavrentiy had said, but they were wild out in the night still, with the fire.

The stones that knuckled into her through the groundsheet and the sleeping bag were like the lumps and folds of the plastic dress lap of the snow queen who had been so fake, except that she could not properly think this. If she did, it made her the same person who had thought of being that other-same child in the marquee at the shopping centre. Valya and Elda would be at the oval of machines at the outdoor gymnasium all weekend, and they would go back to Valya's together. At the moment that was this very moment, her brother would be watching his videos, and her bed was empty in the room. Her portraits in beads were under the bed and the sleeping bag was gone from under her father's. If he noticed it gone, she would need more lies. She was full of lies. She was a sack stitched of lies, like a sleeping bag. She was lying here and lying about being here and not keeping to the plan to be more normal, like Valya. She was lies and also, she really was tired.

At some point, when there was no more guitar, there were rustling figures in the tent. Feet pushed against her like she'd known they would. There was someone rustling who had hair that was a colour that purple and black hair would become in a tent that was dark and now was warmer than before. The rustling stopped from the one with the hair, except for last rustling that came from her feet, close to the almost daughter's ribs.

The almost daughter had beads in her eye-mind.

In the morning, which was really just later in the morning that had started while the van had still been rattling, the tent was empty and cold again.

There was frost. It crisped as the almost daughter tied her boots on over the socks. It crisped as she walked to where the fire had been, and where now the faces were more bleared than glowing. The eyes the almost daughter saw were tight and some were reddened and voices were more hoarse, but the noise and laughs were the same as before. One boy in a felt hat that wrapped his ears and chin was laughing so much that he fell from the stump he was sharing with another boy. Everyone was eating apples, dark bread and cheese, from plates or mostly from their knees.

The almost daughter took the apple and small brick of bread that a man who was holding a knife handed up to her. On the ground in front of him was the boy the almost daughter had sat next to in the van.

Morning, said the boy. Sleep well?

Her mouth was full of bread and chewing. She sat.

No chocolates? said the boy. I could really do with chocolate.

The almost daughter swallowed and the bread globe was close to whole as it entered her throat. I think someone finished my chocolates, she said.

Bastard, said the boy. What a total bastard.

Unbelievable, said the almost daughter.

The bread became easier to chew and swallow. The boy listed his favourite bars of chocolate and milk sweets.

Anyway, he said. Before I drool too much. Which group are you going with today?

The almost daughter pointed to her cheek, where the bread was gone but where her tongue made the shape of the bread still there and blocking her.

I'm going with the digging group, said the boy. His eyes were alive despite the red around them. Can you imagine if we actually found something? he said. Bones or skulls or something. You never know.

The almost daughter nodded. She chewed her tongue, until it could not credibly be bread any more. She said that she would join the other group, for now.

The boy brushed crumbs from the top of his knee. The digging's not for everyone, he said. And it's all important, as long as you're here.

He asked if she was sure she did not have more chocolates. She said she didn't and he made a mock-devastated face. She looked through the face to try to see if she should ask something more about the bones, or to have some idea what the other group was for. He stood and moved across to a girl who was peeling a pastry from transparent wrapping and she had not asked before he moved.

She chewed and then pretended to be chewing, until suddenly there was clapping and the two boys arrived who were the boys from the school who had been in the van. There was Lavrentiy with them next, and the bald girl from the van, and their hair was wet and they had towels at their necks.

Absolute nuts, said the man who had given the almost daughter the bread to eat. So that's where the crazy ones were, he said.

The last of the ones who had arrived and been clapped had a head that was completely covered by a towel. This was the one who came straight to the almost daughter and pulled away the towel, and was dripping from black and purple hair.

You should have come, said Oksana. You're a bit clothed to swim, though.

What happened next was that she hugged the almost daughter, like Lavrentiy had except that her shirt and the towel and her hair were wet. The almost daughter was rigid planks again, or cardboard.

Anyway, I'm glad you're here, said Oksana. I wasn't really sure you'd come. Just make sure you're less clothed tomorrow morning and you can have a proper wash with us.

She had been in the ice of the river and now her arms were around the almost daughter.

You definitely won't need a scarf to swim, she said, and then she pulled herself away and went with Lavrentiy towards the tent. The almost daughter watched him and watched

117

Oksana, who had been naked or nearly naked in the river, and the almost daughter had beads in her eye-mind.

When boots and rucksacks were being tied closed, some-one asked the almost daughter if she was going to be in the painting and signs group. The question did not tell her if this was the same as the group for digging and bones. She looked towards the tent again, where the flaps were still down and no one had come out, and said that she was in the painting and signs group. The woman who had asked gave her a ruck-sack to carry that was bulged with poles of wood and brushes. The poles jutted out from the top of the rucksack and into the almost daughter's neck.

The tent opened and Oksana and Lavrentiy joined a group that was definitely separate now, holding spades.

The almost daughter walked behind the boy who in the van she had heard being spoken to as Toenail. His ears were dirty. They walked through trees, and the poles were heavy and jutting and they walked and walked.

At the place they stopped, there was a clearing in the trees, and wooden poles like the ones from the rucksack were standing upright in the earth. The poles in the rucksack were straight and unbroken, and the poles in the ground were slanted and some were snapped and splintered at the top. The woman who had given the almost daughter the rucksack with the brushes and poles to carry told her to empty it out and get started.

While some of the people tugged the older poles out, others laid the new poles flat and against boards of wood that had been carried as well. Those who had brought nails, and ham-mers, were attaching the boards to the unbroken new poles.

118

A woman who the almost daughter realised was the woman from the fifth floor, and who had spat in the lift, was saying that the boards should be painted first, before the poles were nailed to them.

But for half of them we don't even have names to paint, said the Toenail boy, and the woman said that they should still be painted, even if just in one plain colour, and it was better to do this before the nails.

The nailing and painting and tugging of the old poles was happening around the almost daughter, and she was standing and doing nothing. There was a hammer crooked on the earth near her boots. The last time she had held and tried to use a hammer was when her father had been building the book-case that had space inside it for the new television. At first, the bookcase had not quite had space, because of all the wires that were needed, and she had helped her father to take pieces apart and screw and nail them back together. She had been with her father all day and he had clamped the nails between his teeth until he used them.

She picked up the hammer and it was more of a weight than she had remembered it to be. She bit three nails between her teeth.

The first board took her nearly fifteen minutes to complete. It slid on the pole and she was slow and inaccurate but no one was noticing and she was doing something real. When the board was close to straight on the pole and not loose, and the sharp tips of the two nails were flattened at the back like she had seen the others make them flat, a boy said to her that it looked good and was ready to be painted next.

She said that she could do it and she painted it black, like all the other boards on poles.

She counted 116 of the old poles, when all of them were out of the ground and in a heap. They were heaped and splintered and would be taken away, and there were 130 of the new, replacing poles, which were harder to count because of being nailed and painted and driven into the earth, in different orders but at the same time.

The almost daughter nailed another board and pole, and a third, and she was quicker and she painted them. She beat her thumb with the hammer twice, and this was stupid but her thumb did not bleed much. It was only from the surface and she wiped it away.

She painted black and dense across the boards, and for one of them, the woman who had given her the brushes gave her a name to paint as well. It was to paint on with a thinner brush and in white, and was a name and two years that were birth and death. The woman said that they came from the archive. She said that the reason why one girl was crying as she painted another name from the archive was because the girl was related to the name. Her parents didn't want her to come, she said.

The almost daughter nailed and painted thirteen markers, and added two more names and their years. Her blood was wiped on the backs of the poles. Not on all of them, but on some, and it was there in the beads in rows in her eye-mind.

In the middle of the day, when she had taken off her coat and scarf and was still warm enough inside, from the hammering and from the focus, which was strange and powerful against the cold air, two bags lined with ice packs were opened up. There were more apples, and more dark bread, and cheese, and this time there was sausage and cans as well. There were

120

bottles with the same caps that were under her bed. She took a small knife and cut from the cheese and the sausage, and the sausage tasted more like nuts than real sausage.

The beads in the bottle caps in her eye-mind were all one portrait in the woods. She was threading the black from the painted boards and the dead names in white against the pine green of trees, and against what the woman who had given her the names was now saying about how they had originally known to come and look just here for bones. The woman said that there had always been a rumour that bodies from the main camp were taken to the woods when they disappeared and had been ill or exhausted. There were several different places in the woods. There were beads, tiny, among all the others, for the testimony of one survivor who had said that his logging group had found bodies themselves, and they remembered where in the woods it had been, and later, much later, the bodies were found.

Partly, the almost daughter was listening, and was beading it all and could not help it, and partly, she was nodding when the boy who was Toenail offered her a real bottle with the cap snapped off. Then she was even warmer inside, and she laughed when another boy told her that the sausage really was made from nuts, and mushroom.

In the afternoon, she painted and nailed, with nails in her teeth and the sausage in her teeth, and she helped to clear the space for the extra poles that were not just new because they were replacements, but new because new names had been matched. The fourteen new poles needed new space, and she lifted two huge branches from trees that had fallen already to make the space, with others who were lifting too.

121

The branches could only be moved because of everyone who was lifting at once.

She readied the poles for the photographs that a man in a chequered bandana was taking, because no one was going to come to the woods very often and remember the bodies, but with photos on a website and maybe in the museum, it meant that people could remember them there. The almost daughter was still listening and threading: the museum now was more than just a plan, and the website was already active. The photographs were of markers and of names in the trees, and then some were of the living bodies who had painted and nailed for the bodies not living, and the photographs were portraits as well, in the woods.

She walked back following Toenail and the bald girl, and the broken and old poles were in the rucksack, and the bristles on the brushes were gummed with paint. Her shoulders and arms had the feeling of hammering, which was like the feeling of after the machines outside the Palace of Creativity and Youth, except that it was also a feeling of meaning.

Back near the tents, there was already a fire, and there was meat and the other meat that was mushrooms. There was cheese that was not hard any more, as it was melted on sticks on the grill above the fire, and it was salted and like rubber to chew and wonderful. The almost daughter ate the cheese until her mouth hurt, and drank from another can and fizzed. She moved her lips when there was singing and the two guitars, and sometimes her voice came too. There were more nicknames: there was Snout and Fishscale.

When the second group with spades and dirtied faces came back, their dirtied faces were frowning and hard. Not all of them were hard: some were more like shrugs, and they took cans and cheese and meat on sticks and said that next time, maybe, they would find something. Lavrentiy said he was definitely sure that next time for sure he would definitely find something.

The face under black and purple hair was hard and frowning and also burning. The almost daughter drank more from the can.

She drank more and was singing or not singing and then stood. She took cheese stretched in strings on a stick from the grill and walked to where Oksana's face was flaming.

I'm sorry you didn't find things, she said. The things you were looking for. Where you were looking.

Oksana did not take the cheese on the stick and was not looking at the cheese. What? she said.

The almost daughter pulled her mouth into order. It's sad, she said. It's just sad you didn't find them.

She waited and was not waiting precisely for arms around her like in the morning, but for anything that was not silence and blankness.

Yes, said Oksana. It's sad. Great insight.

The almost daughter held the cheese on the stick that was turning to something now too much like rubber. She had hammered and painted and been part of the day, and what was left was to be part of it with Oksana as well. She wanted to be part of it with Oksana, and now she was congealing and becoming only stupid.

Oksana and her face turned away. They turned and then she had stood and she was crossing to where other frowned faces were. Lavrentiy was there and his face was less hard, and Oksana lowered herself beside him. She put her head on his shoulder and closed her eyes and Lavrentiy tilted his head to hers. Then they were eating meat or not meat together from the same stick that Lavrentiy was holding. Oksana's face was burning with the fire but not hard now. She leaned close to Lavrentiy and the meat or not meat in their mouths came from the stick and mixed, and now she was smiling, even in the shrugged way.

The almost daughter chewed the cheese that was completely rubber and bland elastic and not wonderful. She sat with Toenail and she did not sing. She said to Toenail that she was tired and she went towards the tent with the flaps. She dropped the cheese and stepped on it. Lavrentiy was something the almost daughter was not, or he had done something she could not do, and she had nailed and hammered but still was not part. Beads were drifting out of place in her eye-mind.

In the tent, she was filled with greasy cheese and cans, and this was all she was and she slept. Or she possibly slept, or tried to sleep, and then there was a stone or branch that was under her and spearing into her spine through the groundsheet. She twisted and arched herself away from the stone or root or branch, and it moved with her. She rose inside the worm of the sleeping bag and beneath her but not beneath the groundsheet, after all, was a penknife in a marble casing. She lay back, and with her hands raised, she extracted each of the segments of the knife. There was the neat blade that was sharp and for cutting, and slicing and putting an end to things, and the screwdriver for loosening or escape. There was the toothpick, a nail file, and the spiral of the corkscrew. The spanner slid out just as precisely, and back, and every tiny perfect tool was designed for its specific use and knew exactly what it was for. There was no question and the click was sure, and outside there were the faces at the fire, so glowed, who knew why they were there and could say so. There was the girl who was related to the name and had cried, and the ones who knew that they wanted to find bones. They had come with the whole of themselves and they fit. And further from the tent – much further – were the tools or pieces who knew for certain that they wanted to do modelling and be beautiful women, and have glamour and perfumes and their boyfriends on motorbikes. They were all so definite and properly suited.

The last tool in the knife the almost daughter snapped out was the piece that had no obvious purpose. Her father's pen-knife had the same final segment, not clearly for cutting or coaxing loose or blunting. It was flat with an angle cut out of it and missing. It was there not specifically knowing itself. She was holding the casing with the meaningless tool out and it really was repulsive and entirely pointless, and then she was asleep again.

She woke and at first she was sure that she was still asleep, because of the face. Oksana's face was the face in her face, and it was not the dream form of the face, because this new one was streaked with smoke-dirt. The dirt was under Oksana's left eye and in the dream there had been no dirt.

You're hiding, said Oksana. You're in here and hiding.

I'm sleeping, said the almost daughter.

Oksana rubbed the dirt beneath her eye, and it stayed and was still dirt, except streaked even further. You're not sleeping any more, she said.

The almost daughter pulled up onto the backs of her elbows. There was only Oksana in the tent, and her.

You're hiding here but that wasn't the point, said Oksana. The point is I'm sorry and I wanted you to know.

The almost daughter pushed her elbows harder down, through her sleeves and the sleeping bag and the groundsheet. She could feel the definite earth and was not sleeping.

Oksana stretched sideways and lay over the blankets, not perpendicular, like the night before, but parallel. For before, she said. I guess I was rude. I know I was rude and I didn't want to be, to you. I'm just angry and annoyed and really, really angry.

The almost daughter pressed the earth with her elbows. Because you didn't find stuff with the digging, she said.

We didn't find a single fucking speck, said Oksana. We were digging there for hours and I was sweating like a boar and there was nothing and we really did think it was the place. That woman from the archive was so convinced. They were all so sure and I was too.

The almost daughter nodded and the nod was invisible in the dark.

And then it's not even that I'm angry for that, said Oksana. That doesn't even make sense.

This did make sense to the almost daughter.

We don't exactly want to find bones, said Oksana. Obviously. So we can't be angry. But if we know they're here somewhere then we do want to find them. We have to because otherwise they're totally lost. And that's what makes me angry and I hate it.

The almost daughter nodded and was invisible again. It was not enough to be invisible.

They're not lost, she said.

What? said Oksana.

They're not lost because you're looking for them, she said.

This was now not an invisible thing. It hung in the cave of the tent and waited, and was in the triangular space above. The almost daughter waited and the space waited.

You're right, said Oksana. Okay. You're right. They're not.

Oksana was pushing into her elbows too, and she was up and level with the almost daughter.

I like that, she said. I like how you said that.

It's true, said the almost daughter.

It is true, said Oksana. And I like that. Except that you said *You're looking for them*. You should have said *We*. We're looking for them.

The cave of the tent was high and waiting. I was in the other group, said the almost daughter.

Say it, said Oksana. Say it. Come on.

The other group, said the almost daughter. I wasn't digging anything.

Say it, said Oksana. You're here and we're all here and it's the same so just say it.

The almost daughter was wrapped in the sleeping bag that smelled of her father and under his bed, and she was wrapped in so many layers and casings. And Oksana was saying she was part of something.

They're not lost because we're looking for them, she said.

There, said Oksana. That wasn't so hard.

It was not so hard. It was solid but not hard.

Good, said Oksana. It's good that you've said that.

In the tent cave, it did become solid and good. Digging had been good but so was painting and nailing, and because of the digging and nailing and marking, there were people who were lost who were not completely lost. They were not completely lost, after all.

And it's good that you're here, said Oksana. That was the other thing that's the point. That's what I wanted to come and say too. That it's good that you're here and I'm glad you came.

The almost daughter was wrapped in the sleeping bag that smelled in theory of her father, and now she could not smell at all. She could not see because of the dark: she could not taste or smell or see. But she could hear and she had heard what Oksana had said. She could hear and it was visible.

There was one more thing.

Oksana? said the almost daughter.

Oskana made a sleeping sound.

I need to ask you a question, said the almost daughter.

Oksana turned the sound into something that said that she was close to sleeping but would also listen for one moment more.

The almost daughter thought about her question. It could be made as a question about the feeling of a shapeless tool in a penknife, and the feeling of being almost, always. It was a question to pry out of the casing of the knife and it snagged and was too stiff to come. And it possibly should not come at all: it was not entirely right for the tent, and with the woods and the not-lost people remembered. Except that maybe it did link somewhere, just too far to think about so late.

A question, said the almost daughter. You and Lavrentiy.

Oksana was still and made no sound.

Are you something, together? said the almost daughter.

The sound from Oksana was an explosion. She was exploding with laughter and she was shaking, and the tent was

128

shaking, and the almost daughter was shaking and exploding, too. She was exploding or she was imploding instead.

That's the most hilarious thing I've ever heard, said Oksana, when she had finished the explosion except for small aftershocks, and was able to speak again in full words. No, she said. The answer is No times a thousand.

The almost daughter made a sigh sound of her own that suggested that she was asleep and casual.

And actually, said Oksana. It's good that you know that. Especially you. It's better you know.

The almost daughter turned over with her eyes closed so that she faced Oksana lying right and tight next to her, although she was not truly facing her because of her eyes being closed and hiding.

Oksana did not say anything else. The air made it seem as if she might, but she did not.

Then the almost daughter was facing her because her eyes were not completely closed. They were hiding but between the lashes she could see. She could see through dark and maybe further. Oksana had said it was good that she had come, and Oksana had said: Especially. The bodies in the forest were not completely lost, and through eyelashes and dark they were still just there. There were so many and some had markers painted and some did not have painted, nailed markers. Not yet, and Oksana had said: Especially.

The beads in the next day of the portrait held a charge. The almost daughter woke too late to swim, but Oksana had also woken too late. She was lying, still so close and parallel, and her hair was soft and curved into her eyes instead of spiking out like it did in the daytime. Lavrentiy shook her awake and she groaned, and he had been to the river and come back. He shook the almost daughter by her shoulders and she was awake already but groaned too. Outside in the circle around the gone fire, there was cheese again and bread that now was stiffer even than before, and then it was soft and delicious because someone had made the huge kettle work, finally, and there was tea and sugar for the bread to melt into. This was what some of the flood-charge was made of. Oksana brought the almost daughter a tea glass with a chip in the rim and the almost daughter began to drink, until Oksana saw the chip and swapped it for the glass that she had had between her feet, and which she had already held to her mouth. This was what some of the charge was made of.

When the groups divided, Oksana picked up a spade and then said that her arms were aching. She lifted a bag of the brushes instead that may or may not have been equally heavy, and the almost daughter lifted the bag of brushes she had carried before, and it had poles but fewer poles than before. Lavrentiy raised his eyebrows at Oksana and she skewered his arm with a brush from the bag. In the walking, the almost daughter was not next to Oksana, but she was behind the boy whose name was Snout and he was walking next to Oksana. She was close enough to hear Oksana telling him about the teacher who was always drunk at the previous school that she had been to. She performed the way the teacher slurred and staggered, and this meant that she slowed and the almost daughter was closer.

At the new stopping point between the trees, there were not as many wooden poles in the earth. The boards that were attached to them were painted not with names but information, and some had objects nailed or glued on. It was not a

130

place where bones had been found but was a place that two women said had been a sub-camp that was temporary and not the main site, and the buildings were gone but the objects had been left. The objects were tools and machinery, and a bracelet. The almost daughter re-painted and re-nailed, and Oksana and everyone re-painted and re-nailed, and then it was time to use the nails for something new. It was like a bird-house or a miniature cabin on four poles, and Oksana held one of the poles to keep it steady as the almost daughter nailed it to the platform.

When it was ready and it was lined with metal sheets that also had been carried through the woods, the women who had described the sub-camp positioned a fat, rounded candle inside it. They lit it and there was a circle around it, and it was not like the circle for the fire and the sausage, because the candle was for the people in the sub-camp who had been here and then had no more records. They were bones and unnamed bodies or had been sent somewhere else, but they were not lost, completely, because of the searching and Oksana had said that this was true. The circle was quiet. The candle was bright. The almost daughter and Oksana and all of the hands had built the house for the candle and the lives that had no ending that was known.

And then someone looked at a watch and swore, and they packed the backpacks and blew out the flame, and took photographs quickly and went back through the trees, sometimes walking and sometimes running and tripping. At the tents, they stuffed and rolled sleeping bags and rucksacks, and then the almost daughter was in the van at the window. Oksana was climbing into a car with Lavrentiy and the boy with a tattoo on the back of his neck, and she looked through the glass to the almost daughter and made a heart shape with her hands that pointed at Lavrentiy.

The charge of the portrait was the sugar and the tea, and when Oksana had made the almost daughter speak out loud, but it was also from the candle in the birdhouse. It was a through-charge that was not just sweet but was real. It stayed in the van, through the trees and on the tracks, and then on the roads of people who were coming from the houses in the country with toilets in huts. It stayed even on the tarmac at the beginning of the town. The man in the chequered bandana in front of her was looking at the photographs of the marker poles and boards and the candle on the camera he had, and deciding which to show on the website. This is the portrait of things becoming distinct.

On the bus from where she left the van, where she had also been waiting two nights before, the magic charge and the candlelight melted. They still hovered in the background at first, as there were others on the bus who had come from the van, but there was not the music there had been in the van, and not the laughing or the serious talking either. The man who had been checking the photographs kept his camera zipped in its case, and looked at the crack in the seat in front like he was just a man on a bus at night without a camera and without his choices. The almost daughter said goodbye to him at her stop, and he nodded and studied the crack again. In the lift, she was not just moving up to the twelfth floor of the building from the ground: it was the whole weekend and the real distinctness dropping further beneath her and out of her, floor by floor.

Inside the apartment, her mother was speaking to the woman in Bristol in the box on the screen, and it meant that her father was working a night shift. The woman in Bristol was saying that she often confused the words that were for church and circus, and her mother was saying that in fact it was not just the words that could easily be confused. When the almost daughter properly came into the room, her mother stopped laughing at what she had said and her head moved to cover the almost daughter behind her. She then moved her head again and said: My daughter. She was having a holiday this weekend.

The woman in Bristol asked where she had been, and the almost daughter's mother said she had been staying with a friend in another town. She did not say anything about planting and vegetables, and the woman in Bristol waved with her hand. Behind the woman it was bright in the sky still, and it would have been a time of day when the almost daughter had still been in the van, or even still packing or tripping on the tree roots. Her mother was now saying to the woman that it was nice to go away for the weekend sometimes. There was not a single time the almost daughter could remember when her mother had gone away for the weekend.

She pushed the sleeping bag under the father's bed and wondered if it smelled of fire and meat and sausages not made of meat. In the bedroom, her brother did not say that she smelled of fire in her hair or her clothes. He said that she smelled of wet earth and toilet.

I saw a spider in the hut that looked like you, she said.

That's how much you missed me, he said.

She did not ask what he had been doing since the Friday. Every word and every step of being back and inside was taking the fires and the candle even further. He said, when she still had not asked, that he had been to a martial arts club with

133

Yevgeniy. She said that she hoped they would knock each other out.

She stood under the spitting showerhead and remembered things and tried not to, at once. The others would be washing the woods from their skin, too. Toenail and Snout and the woman who lived on the fifth floor would be doing this, and the man with the bandana would, and he would have his photographs to show. Oksana's hair would be black in the water, but the purple would really still be there. Far away, but not so far, there were markers and a birdhouse on poles in the dark.

Portrait #28
The woman with the cave inside her

The woman with the cave gored inside her waits. She has been waiting and nothing and no one has come. The door has not key-clicked for her since – when? She has waited and the longest crack in the far wall has become a river and a vein and a noose. The cabbage leaves left are collapsed and soft, and frail like weak hands and they are not to be looked at. The woman with the cave inside her does not want these muted hands.

When no one comes, it is so often time only to wait, but just now it is time also to think of the wax thing. Just now because of the ripeness she is feeling. Just now it builds in her and swells. What should be done is that the wax thing should be placed in its holder, which is made of clay and is somewhere – must be – and it should be lit at its tip where there is string. There should be the photograph. She wants this. She wants stronger hands to place and light.

The woman with the cave inside waits with these should-things, and the photograph is somewhere and the wax thing is somewhere. And matches should and will be needed to scrape the flame into life for the wax thing, but the matches are not even somewhere. They are finished. She knows this. The last of them has ashed away to nothing, and she could or should ask the ghost of the ghost of the atrocious ghost to bring more for her, or ask the ghost of the ghost of the ghost of the ghost, if she is the one who comes more now, but neither of them have come in the waiting. No one has come and then perhaps she should not ask because perhaps the wax thing is just a sense-less, liar thing. It says *life* when the flame comes, when there really is no life. It says *remember* when there is too much to remember. She should and she could but she will not find the wax, and she will not believe in the lies of the flame life. The cabbage leaves collapse and the should-things collapse. Weak hands. Only weak and drained, numb hands, and their traces of the blisters and scars and cold, and they will not reach for anyone today.

Remember what? Remember when something. Remember in a room, a secret—

Wait a little. Wait and ash.

Part IV

Part IV

Portrait #29
Back to / Speak to

It was only on the way to school, walking with her brother and then also with Yevgeniy, that the almost daughter read the messages on her phone that had come from Valya and Elda at the weekend. Now she saw that they had asked if she was tying her hair into a scarf to do the planting, and if she had found a husband with no teeth. Clearly she has, Valya had written. If she's not replying they're married already. Elda had written: Six children already, and Valya had written: And none of them have teeth. After this, they had written twenty messages of plans for where to meet on the Sunday morning, and then more describing a girl who was fat sitting close to them in the cafe they had chosen. She looked like she'd eaten her mother, Valya had written. And then a bison for dessert.

In the classroom, when the almost daughter came to Valya's desk, where Elda was already, they stopped talking and left a pause that was to show that they had been talking and stopped.

So you deigned to come back to the civilised world, said Valya, after there had been enough pause.

You have time for us after all, said Elda. You left your husband milking the cows, or what?

No, said Valya. He left her. He left her for a cow, I'm thinking.

Elda made a retching sound.

It's true, said Valya. They actually do that.

There weren't any cows, said the almost daughter. There were potatoes and chickens and carrots but not cows.

Valya and Elda looked at each other.

Oh, said Valya. So a carrot, not a husband. You mean a giant dildo carrot.

That's what was keeping you so distracted, said Elda.

The almost daughter thought about making the retch sound, but Elda made it first and she could not. The reception was just bad there, she said. The signal.

When the bell came and the teacher walked into the room, she waited for Elda to move to her desk before she left to go to hers.

I need to tell you something, she said to Valya.

Valya nodded. Later on, she said.

There was just one point in the rest of the day, between geometry and computer technology, when the almost daughter saw Oksana. The room with the computers was on the ground floor, and while the almost daughter's class were taking down their bags, Oksana's class was coming up. The almost daughter realised this before she saw Oksana herself. She slowed and held her hand on the railing and the others pushed ahead of her, and the railing, rubber gummed around metal, failed to decide for her what to do. If she said anything, someone could

140

hear, and someone could be Elda or Valya or anyone, and either way, her voice might not come. If she said nothing, she would be smothering something, and the fire and the candle would be wiped out completely.

She was slow until she had nearly stopped, and most of the other class had reached and passed her. The railing had still refused to help and she really was going to do nothing at all, or she would twitch her head, which no one would see, and Oksana, equally, would not see. She was going to walk past and sit in front of a computer for an hour and make pages link together, when nothing for her was linking together, and then Oksana was five steps below. She was not the very last but she was close to the last. She was just one step below and she was crouching down and tying a shoelace that was tied already. She was holding a perfect bow in her fingers.

You look cool today, she said. And anyway, take this.

She spoke straight down to the tied and bowed lace and she stood and grinned to the air in front of her. She passed and climbed the final steps, not rushing, and the almost daughter moved her hand from the rail. She bent to fake-tie her own shoelace on the step, and pulled free what had just been inserted between the shoe wall and her inner ankle. It had felt like a secret slipping, and delicate. It was paper and delicate and electric at once. In the room with the computers, she could still feel it in her.

They went to the oval of machines at the back of the Palace after the end of lessons. Valya timed thirty seconds on her phone for doing as many sit-ups as possible on the steel sheet with a bar that both feet could tuck under, and then she timed sixty seconds, and two minutes. She timed three minutes for the most painful version, when the right elbow had to cross

141

to the left knee on the way up, and the left elbow had to cross to the right knee. The knees were not supposed to move: only the elbows were allowed to move, and Valya wrote the numbers down in her notebook. She said the competition was a self-competition and not for comparing against each other, but she also circled the sixty-second numbers, when she had not done the most and the almost daughter had.

When she had written down times for calf raises too, and shown her stomach lines and where she said they still were not right, she leafed back to the page at the front of the notebook. She asked if Elda and the almost daughter were remembering to use the photographs that she had glued for them as inspiration.

Elda said that of course she was, and that hers was a motivation like an angel, and the almost daughter could not gauge exactly if sarcasm was in her voice.

Good, said Valya. Yours especially. I saw she's just been in commercials in Taiwan.

Totally, said Elda. Motivational.

And? said Valya. What about yours? Or is the cow-humping husband your guiding light now?

Yes, said the almost daughter. Or no. Yes to the photograph and no to the husband.

Valya nodded and flattened her eyes.

And do you talk to her every night like we said? she said.

The almost daughter looked at Valya. Talk to the photograph? she said.

To the photograph, said Valya.

We said we would, said Elda.

The almost daughter could not remember this, and at the same time she could very much believe it. There were the rituals that Valya had devised for dedication, like chewing mouthfuls

142

forty-four times and thinking always of New York and Milan in the shower.

Yes, said the almost daughter. Pretty much every night. Just to tell it what we're doing. Tell her.

Elda was still looking at Valya, but Valya was looking at the almost daughter.

Pretty much every night, said Valya. You open the notebook and you speak to the photograph?

More or less, said the almost daughter. Mostly.

Well, that's pretty weird, isn't it? said Valya.

The almost daughter pressed her nails into the palms of her hands.

To be talking to a fucking paper photograph, said Valya. Every single night. Is it like you're obsessed with her or something? Is that who you picture your carrot thing is?

Elda snapped her head up and laughed in high pitch. God, it was a joke! she said. You're obsessed. We were fucking joking! she said.

The almost daughter nodded and said: Thanks for the clarification.

It was still not clear if this had been an idea that was planned in advance, or if Valya had been seized by creativity in the moment. It could have been in the cafe, with the girl they said was fat, or maybe there had been no girl, and the cafe, even, had been a decoy. They could have been anywhere and planning for anything. When Valya said that the almost daughter maybe really did speak to the photograph, and asked her what the photograph said in return, the almost daughter said she was in fact very talkative. She said that the girl had promised her that she would fly her plane to collect her and save her from the losers she was stuck being friends with.

Elda's eyes said that the almost daughter was still not permitted to be part of the joke, but Valya's eyes were back on the pages of the notebook and the numbers in it. She said that they would do the sit-ups and the leg raises again in a week, and she said that it was vital to improve. She said that she did not mean important: she meant vital. For the almost daughter it had been important before to say what she was going to say to Valya. It had been important as soon as the questions had come about the husband and the stupid cows and thick carrots, and now it was vital, too.

Elda said that she would have to leave, and she stood for Valya to come with her to the tram, and Valya stayed high on the ellipsis machine. Elda waited a minute more, and then said to the almost daughter not to forget to kiss her photograph goodnight. She looked to Valya a last time, and left.

The almost daughter sat down on the stretch of rubber that spanned between two rolls of metal on the treadmill structure that did not work. She was close to the ellipsis machine with only the wooden bars in between, and she was ready to speak to Valya immediately. It was better to be quick before other thoughts came.

But Valya was first. You had something to say, she said. And I really hope it's an apology, for your sake.

The almost daughter listed apologies in her mind. There was apology for not replying to the messages all weekend, and for smelling of dirt and farm when she came back, and for being idiotic and gullible enough to believe that talking to a photograph that was printed and glued inside a notebook was a good idea and serious. There was a vast rubber stretch of possible apologies but she had to choose the right one among them.

144

I don't know, said Valya. I just don't know what to make of it. I can't believe you could just forget.

There was something else that was some other weight on the rubber, then. The almost daughter ran and ran for it and was nowhere.

And you still can't remember, or what, said Valya.

She stepped down from the long ellipsis pedals and came to the broken and useless treadmill. She raised one foot onto the stretch of rubber and it bobbed to make the almost daughter jerk upwards.

The portfolio? This weekend? said Valya. Collecting it? Ring any bells at all?

The treadmill was broken and had never been motorised, but now it was doing the thing from videos where the rubber kept moving while her face was down, skinning away the flesh from her and making her bleed and crumple at its edge.

It's literally like you don't care, said Valya, and next she would say that she should have known that she should have taken Elda all along. Now there was only one way to clamber up. It had been important and then vital, and now it was the only way and needed more, too.

That's it, said the almost daughter. That's really what I needed to tell you.

What? said Valya. This had better be good.

The almost daughter bent forward to her backpack and zipped open the pocket at the front, with the keyring. She pulled out paper first, which was the wrong thing to pull, and then she pulled out card, which was right.

When we went to the shoot for the portfolio, she said. This – I didn't really know if it was true, but—

Valya grabbed at the card from her. What in the hell is this? she said.

One of the men at the shoot, said the almost daughter. It's his, and he said he might have something for us.

Valya's eyes stayed on the card and the phone number. For us? she said.

Yes, said the almost daughter. He said: You and your friend, the tall one. He must have seen us outside, together.

The almost daughter told Valya what the man from the back of the marquee in the jacket had said to her about her face. She said true parts and invented parts. She said that the man had definitely wanted her friend to know and come as well.

This is huge, said Valya, and it was working.

I just, said the almost daughter. Needed to think.

Valya shook her head and said twice more that it was huge and that it could really now change everything. She asked the almost daughter again to repeat what the man in the marquee had said, about her face and in his own exact words. She was saying nothing about carrots and obsessions now, and the way she asked was sometimes something that was like admiring, but maybe shocked, too. She showed the almost daughter the envelope of photographs that was her portfolio and the almost daughter said that they were stunning.

She gave the almost daughter a second envelope. I picked yours up too in the end, she said. Even if you don't actually care, with you turning heads without it now.

Valya said that she should call the man in either three or four days' time to show that they were interested but not desperate.

And this really could be what we need, she said.

The almost daughter held the envelope and tasted the admiration again.

Portrait #30
And speak

At the apartment, her mother said that her brother was at the martial arts club again. The almost daughter said that she would do her homework later and closed the bedroom door.

The envelope of the portfolio photographs, the business card that was from the man, and the paper that had made her foot privately glitter and the whole of her body privately glitter: she laid them on the bed to form a line. Her hand moved to the paper and she stopped it. She blurred her eyes to the card so that she would not see the phone number properly.

She placed the notebook in the line as well. The notebook had been in the pile that was next to the bed and this, she opened. She wrote the numbers of the sit-ups that she could remember and soon, she could not remember. The ones she could remember best were Valya's. She returned back through the notebook to the first page, inside the cover.

I did it to save things, she said to the photograph. I did it to make her like me again and not think about being so disgusting and weird.

Her voice was small and artificial, and the photograph was flat and pathetic and said nothing. What the almost daughter needed and wanted to say was more than this, and connected to more. At the school, in the room with the computers, the websites to make were basic and plain and were really only text in different sizes, but the way they linked was complicated. If you were linked to too many things it was a mess, and clicking on one could be unreliable and take you somewhere you were not prepared for. There was no sitemap and the teacher in the room with the computers said that the crucial constant was the sitemap.

The famous girl or woman or whatever she was in the notebook was hearing nothing. If she said anything back, she was saying: Can't help you. She had a smile that was not a smile but a pout. The beads, this time, might not be enough either: it was something else that had to be done.

When the almost daughter's brother came back, he had sweat in his hair and pink across his cheeks. He showed her the self-defence kicks he had learned and they looked more like they were offence than defence. She told him this and he said that their mother had said she had heard her talking to herself, in the bedroom, like an insane total nut.

In the bathroom, as she brushed her teeth, the sleeping bag was drying, above the tub. It was not underneath her father's bed, where it should have been.

It stank, said her brother, when he came and stood behind her. He said their mother had said she needed to wash it.

*

Sixteen portraits. There they were. There was powerful face, and vengeful face, and the four melancholy versions of face. And crossed arms and opened legs and dark eyes. Who were they? Who were they almost but not quite? Portraits in one envelope, and a card, and folded and still not unfolded paper.

Portrait #31
The woman with the cave inside her

The woman with the cave inside her, crag-sore inside her and gnarled inside her, is collecting the blackened-burnt match things from the floorboards. She must have found them and they were not finished after all, though it is true she does not remember the finding. Whatever happened when she did find and scrape and light them and watch them shiver, without the wax thing, is now gone: it is now these char-crisp pieces of spent wood. She certainly cannot have found the wax thing, because if she had then wax would be spotted in solid drips on the floorboards as well, along with the crisp black matches and their flakes. She is collecting them from the floorboards in shavings and gathering them on one of the plates. It is a small plate for underneath a cup, and patterned, and the cup is gone too or she never had it. Now, the matches are definitely finished.

Her hand jolts the plate and the flake pieces rain. She will sigh and no one will hear her sigh and she will have to lower and start again. Gather.

She is not surprised, this time, by the key-click. It makes her jump, and yes, makes the plate fall, again, and the matches in pieces spatter once more, but this is only because of the noise. What she is not surprised by is the fact of the key-click, because she has been waiting for it. In a buttoned inward way, she has been waiting.

The ghost of the ghost of the ghost of the ghost, again, and she is not surprised. It is something else she feels. She is warm and alight.

The ghost of the ghost of the ghost of the ghost sets the vegetables down and does not look at the sink. She looks at the plate on its face on the floorboards and the scatter pieces of matches around it. Oh, that's – she says, and she says she has brought something.

First, though, she says she needs to speak. She needs to say some things and she needs to say them to the woman with the cave inside her. After that, she wants to ask some things and she says this is the important part.

She says that this is vital as well, and here she stops and holds up a small card. I thought this was vital, too, she says. Or it is. Maybe it is, she says.

The woman with the cave inside her does not understand the whole of what the ghost of the ghost of the ghost of the ghost says about the small rectangle card. She tries, and some of it, she does understand. She understands that the ghost of the ghost of the ghost of the ghost has to make a telephone call to the person whose name is tiny on the card, and that she is afraid and also determined.

I just need for them not to be laughing at me, she says. And saying what they say about – about – and I can't be the freak who doesn't want to do this stuff.

She says: I still think in a kind of way it could make me more how I'm meant to be.

She turns the card in her ghost hands. Do you see? she says.

The woman with the cave inside her is nodding because she does know how it is to want to be liked and not strange. She knows how it is to have wanted and tried to be what she, a she-woman, should supposedly be. Without any cave. So: Yes, she says.

The ghost of the ghost of the ghost of the atrocious ghost is quiet, and then she says: Thank you. She sits on the floorboards with the card in her hands and is sitting on top of the splitters of matchsticks. She brings four of the longer pieces into a box shape, and says that it is like a frame and like a kind of picture of something. She breaks the box apart with her fist-back. She looks at the card a last time and slides it away and into the pocket of her coat.

Next, she has something from inside her shoe. It is paper and not card and has handwriting on it, not printed and same-sized letters and numbers.

Then there's this, she says. I just still don't know. I was thinking that maybe you—

Maybe you—

She says tent and bodies and she says the forest. She says markers and remnants and museum and archive. She says: You. She says: The things you were trying to tell me before, with the sculptures out of ice and when – and maybe you and – you – you and – and she says too many things at too much speed. She says something about a tent and how close. The

152

woman with the cave inside her is sloping away and dipping, lapse-sinking, and the ghost of the ghost of the ghost of the ghost does not see this at first and then does.

She stops and says: Sorry. Not yet. Maybe next—

But this, she says. This is for now.

She reaches into the backpack she has and this is impossible and something is mad, because out of the backpack and now in her hand is a box that is real and not a shaped frame of black-burnt. It is a box of the kind that the woman with the cave inside her was going to ask her to bring, except that she did not ask, she is sure. Because the match things are finished and now the ghost of the ghost of the ghost of the atrocious ghost has brought a fresh box of pristine, new matches.

And also from the backpack: she has brought a wax thing. New and wax and thin and shell-white and it will not last long but here it is, and she has brought this wax thing unasked as well. She says something about a birdhouse in forest but what matters is this eggshell wax that is here.

The ghost of the ghost of the ghost of the ghost lights the candle with the matches and is silent now. The woman with the cave inside her has a candle: has what? This ghost-flame. They sit together. They watch together. One of the words from the ghost of the ghost of the ghost of the ghost was forest. A ghost-word.

The ghost of the ghost of the ghost of the ghost tilts the mirror from the wall. Brass hook. Flame in the mirror and the window. Hands behind the mirror hook and touch. Remember – hands. Remember – a voltage.

Portrait #32
Exclamation mark

It was a fact that it would have been possible, theoretically, to send a message to Oksana's phone before the almost daughter had unfolded the paper that had secretly shivered at the inside of her foot when she had bent to false-tie her laces on the staircase. She could have used the messages from Oksana that had been sent to both of the classes in the year group. These were the messages that did not come with words but were videos of the portraits inside the lifts, or images of the president riding a horse that was edited to be a unicorn instead. The almost daughter knew exactly and her fingers knew exactly that if she had clicked on any of these messages, Oksana's number would be shown and so would the option to send a message that was private and would only be seen by her. Her fingers knew what it was to tap so lightly and come to the empty and private blinking space, and then to touch away again quickly, because it would be completely perverse to communicate in this way unbidden.

The number on the unfolded paper made things different, and so did the exclamation mark that was messy-drawn inside a triangle. You're coming with us next time, said the paper. Next time will be just one more meeting and then it's the museum and the actual barracks. You're ready for it, said the paper.

And the number, the triangle, the exclamation mark, and a scribble at the bottom to ignite the pen.

The almost daughter thought of a lone lit wick, and tapped the digits without having to start from the messages to everyone.

See you there, Oksana typed back. It was late at night but it was private, and there were dots to show that more words would appear. They disappeared. They wriggled again. I knew you'd be ready and you are, said the words. And I actually can't wait to see you, they said.

The almost daughter clamped back her hand from writing anything else to reply. The electric shiver was everywhere. Stop that.

Portrait #33
Quilt

It was the same cracked screen to touch, of course, when Valya counted down from ten and it was time to call the man from the marquee. She counted once and the almost daughter pressed the first three numbers from the card, and then she stopped and lowered the phone. She was sitting on Valya's quilt in her bedroom, and Elda was alone and not there.

I don't know, she said.

What? said Valya, and the almost daughter shrugged at her.

Valya said that no one had ever got anywhere being tame and boring. She said that she would essentially do anything, and she said she was tired of repeating herself. She counted down from ten again, and the almost daughter keyed the numbers.

Who is this? said the voice that came. It was a voice that was wearing the man's leather jacket, coarse and reeking of animal and meat.

156

You gave me your card, said the almost daughter. The voice she spoke with wore the blanket of indifference and muted flirtation that she had planned for. She had devised it from how Valya had said she should speak, and from what she also thought would work. At the shoot for the portfolio, she said. She gave her name and the shopping centre's name.

I need a bit more than a name, said the man. If you knew how many honey-sweet girls I see. But that's a different story, I guess.

The almost daughter waited for the laugh that turned into guttered coughing to come to its end. The one with the melancholy eyes, she said.

Valya raised one eyebrow high.

The man made a noise that was not a cough, but also came from his throat, like a groan. You should have said, he said. I remember you, for sure.

I'm interested, said the almost daughter. What you said you might have for me to do. I'm interested.

Valya's second eyebrow met the first. She tilted her palm towards herself and this was the part that could still go wrong.

We're interested, said the almost daughter. It's me and my friend. We're both interested.

Who's your friend? said the man. Is she sensual?

Yes, said the almost daughter. She knew that she should say something more but she could not think of more to say. The man was laughing or coughing again.

If she was having to use her tongue, let's say, he said. Would she be fine with that, for example?

The almost daughter looked at Valya's eyebrows and expecting face. She had not heard. She surely had not heard. The man was joking, but not completely.

Yes, said the almost daughter, and this again was not enough. She'd love it, she said. And so would I.

The man laughed but not so fully that it built into the coughing heave. The almost daughter waited to hear if he was laughing at her or laughing because he was satisfied with what she had said.

I'm sure we can find something perfect for you both, he said. Something we can all enjoy.

The almost daughter gestured an upwards thumb to Valya and felt it inside her fist too. There would be things to have to think about later, but for now she had saved herself from something and Valya would not mention the cows or the carrots, or staring at the girl in the photograph too much, and Elda was the one less committed, again. She wrote down the address and the time that the man gave.

Easy, she said, when the voice had gone.

Valya nodded. Not bad at all, she said.

She asked what the almost daughter had meant about the melancholy eyes, and the almost daughter said that this was what the man had said to her before.

What did he say about me? said Valya.

The almost daughter thought in a way that looked as if she was trying to remember. I can't remember exactly, she said.

Valya blinked and it was there again. It was envy and respect at once, and not anger or mocking or disgust. She breathed in and asked if the man had said it was going to be a shoot for something. The almost daughter said he had, and it did not matter, for now, that he had not. It did not matter about his throat sounds and how far he was joking in what he had said. Valya switched on the television and they watched people racing and competing in a pool of foam and then a pool of red soup, and Valya was glancing at the almost daughter. She was looking for the melancholy, maybe. She had a television that was only hers in a bedroom that was only hers, but she was looking for what the almost daughter had herself. The blanket quilt was an armour around her.

Portrait #34
Portrait in strengths

On the tram from where Valya lived with her mother and her television and her wardrobe of right clothes, the almost daughter sat close to the back. This made it easier to stand and leave if anyone began to ask for tickets. It also should have been easier to leave when her brother's friend Yevgeniy was suddenly in the tram. It should have been easy. It would have been easy. She could have waited for another tram and avoided Yevgeniy and his bulked armpit smell.

She waved her hand up, and called his name.

He pretended to punch his ticket, like she had, and came to sit across the aisle.

Your brother wasn't there, he said.

Where? said the almost daughter.

At the martial arts club, he said. It was good today. One guy had me right round the neck but I did the axe strike thing we were learning and got him down and flat on the floor.

160

He made a sound effect with his throat and slammed his palm into the seat rest in front, and she said Great, and he said that it was.

He picked at the sticker on the back of the seat that was already grained and torn in stripes. He said that she should tell her brother he'd missed out.

The almost daughter opened her mouth to tell him she was sure that her brother had found enough to do all evening, alone with every single video and website at his fingertips. Yevgeniy would roll his eyes at her and mutter and she would be her brother's irrelevant little sister, and this was precisely what she was, except that she was also the person who had spoken to the man on the phone, and made him laugh and cough and give his own throat sounds. And Valya had said: Look at you, turning heads.

I'll tell him, she said. But he'll be way behind now.

Yevgeniy picked loosely at the sticker and essentially had not heard her at all.

I don't think he's been doing as much as you, I mean, she said.

He kept his hands on the seat back and looked at her, unless he was looking past to the window.

Just you can really tell you've been working out, or whatever, even through your coat, she said.

Yevgeniy dropped his hand. His face skittered briefly, through confused and alarmed and then to plumped pride.

I don't know. It's only been a few weeks, he said.

I'm serious, said the almost daughter.

It worked because of course it worked. He recounted more of his strikes and throws and punches and calculated comeback successes, and slowly he pulled the jacket from his arms.

161

They were the arms that had played chess with her brother since they were six or seven years old, unchanged, and still she could force her eyes to move from his and back to the shoulders as if she was transfixed. She could use a force and before the stop where the almost daughter knew that he would leave, she said: Can I? and: Just to feel the difference? Her hand was where his bicep was, or what his belief had swollen into.

Damn, she said. I knew it. I told you.

She was making the melancholy in her eyes, and Yevgeniy cleared his throat and was sweating. I need to get out here, he said. Obviously. I mean, I live here.

See you around, said the almost daughter.

Yes, said Yevgeniy. Maybe. Definitely.

He pushed past her in the aisle and leaned to touch her, not too much, but more than needed.

See you around, he said at the doors. You just said that. Sorry. But still.

He was on the kerb and then receding and she was the one who had made him so fumbling. She could see him checking his shoulders again with his hands as he adjusted his sleeves outside, and this was what she would tell Elda and Valya, or maybe she would tell only Valya, except that she would leave out the part that made it clear that she had spoken first. Her hand had been so close to his armpit, and probably would smell of him, but Valya had said once or more than once that Yevgeniy really was not bad.

She was floating with something, held up by the blanket that had strengthened her voice on the phone to the man. She had the folded, unfolded, and now refolded paper back in her shoe again but it did not fit with anything. At the apartment, in the bathroom, the sleeping bag was gone.

162

Portrait #35
The woman with the cave inside her

The woman with the cave inside her scrapes the long stick thing that is a match, and this is the third scrape of this match and so: flame. She has been lighting the wax thick candle every night now, at the time that the streetlamps outside switch on. She must not let the wax weep too long. It will melt to puddle too fast if she does and then she will have to wait for another, and she does not know if one will come. Maybe someone will come, and bring her more of what she needs, and maybe not.

And the photograph. This time, the photograph. It was there behind the hook of the mirror after all, even if this makes no drop of sense because she has already checked so often. She did not check properly then, or she only dreamed that she had checked but had not.

Now she can see. She can look at the photograph. Not this too long either and not too close, because a photograph does

not melt to puddle but scalds. It catches and burns not to puddle but to shards. Not too long because – not too long. Not too
long because of the hurt of it.

The photograph is one lone face and is the kind of singled
photograph that is just for one face and has its own name. The
type of photograph has a name and the face of course has a
name as well, but without a name, even, still it is a face. Eyes
certainly not to look at too long. Eyes that sear the crevice
inside her and are bright and aching both at once.

The eyes are what take her spinning now. What spins her
now; what thrashed her all the years. However cold and shivered and cursed she was in winters, knowing that the one with
ached eyes was colder, shivering more, more bone-cursed.
What she had to do with the ached eyes and hands, as far as
she would say in the letters that arrived. But how to imagine?
How really to know? Hands rawed red and ears rawed violet,
and ragged cloth around hands to protect them but minced
and lashed and open-scoured anyway. The dragging of logs
and hauling of logs and thunder of logs and heaving of logs.
Drag to the trucks and barking: Faster! and Load! How to hear
it? Like this? Like this? Rags in twists around hands to protect
means no rag left to wrap around feet and so blisters and welts
and more of the raw.

What else in the letters that came from the ghost? The
woman behind her and dragging the logs who used to sing
her song from the fields, in the first weeks or months and
then sang nothing more. The other woman who fell with the
logs and thundered down and could not stand, blood-hands
in blood-snow and screamed the names of her daughters. All
screams and groans in the nights in the bunks, for daughters
and child sons and husbands and mothers. And the woman

164

in the bunk pressed beside her, who says that all of them will starve, or freeze to bone, or work to bone.

And the name I call out for is yours, says the letter.

Until the letters stopped arriving.

When the ghost of the ghost of the ghost of the ghost who comes with the matches and candles does come, and does ask, she tells her, just a little, about the letters. Only three letters, she says. And then nothing.

But how did she get them out? says the ghost of the ghost of the ghost of the lost-eyes ghost.

What she has to say. What the letters had hinted. Something with a guard with a matted moustache who could take letters and messages and even brought food. Bread and once, dark meat and sweet berries. What he wanted in exchange, from the ghost.

I thought, says the ghost of the ghost of the ghost of the ghost. I thought she maybe— I knew.

The only thing she really had, says the woman with the cave inside her. The way she had to survive, she says.

Another version of protection, says the ghost of the ghost of the ghost of the ghost.

Both of them now with the photograph and candle, and the ghost so lone-cursed cold and rawed. In a bunk in the low room of wood and screamed fear. The only way. A kind of chance. The name of the type of photograph is portrait. Portrait. Portrait of a ghost and this cave ache.

To have known a ghost as well as this.

Portrait #36
Permissions

There were three more messages from Oksana before the day that the meeting would be. One message was to remind the almost daughter to look at the website and the photographs from the forest, and the almost daughter had already done this. She had sat in her bed and seen the picture of herself, or at least of one self, with the paintbrush in her hands. She saw the others with their spades, and the campfire, and the markers. The paintbrush was held inside the hand that was holding the screen that was now showing the photographs. So this was her: her body and self. The second message was twenty-eight exclamation marks, and there was also a morning at the school when Oksana had passed the almost daughter in the corridor. Oksana had done the wink thing, and the almost daughter had looked downwards, and she had turned around and Oksana was still there. It was strange to know that a person could feel the redness of a face from inside of it, and to know that it was not just a redness of embarrassment. The third message came ten minutes after this, and was thirty-one exclamation marks. The almost daughter had not responded. She had been to the training with Valya and with Elda every day they went, behind the old Palace of Creativity and Youth. This was a bodyself as well, and churning.

In the underground room below the Palace, at the right time and on the right evening, the windows were still high and thin, and it was interesting that a person's mind could try to focus only on these. It could be automatically calculating how to come through them on days when it rained, and cover was needed from the outdoor machines. A ladder would have to be used, or a rope. Valya would say that a rope was undignified.

These were the things that the narrow windows could be used to lead a mind away to, but inside the windows were the closer things. The seats were filling, though gaps were still there, and Meatflea said hello, and Snout said hello, and Fish-scale gripped up his fist in the air. The almost daughter said hello and raised her fist back, and Oksana was in a row to the left, between Lavrentiy and the girl whose head was shaved. Oksana waved and it was possible that she was going to wink as well, but she did not and the almost daughter waved.

The man with the broken briefcase who had come to the school with the photographs spoke first. He was standing so that his head and body matched perfectly over the head and body of the painted woman in the mural behind.

He said that he was proud of everyone who had been to the forest with the vans and the tents. He said that they showed that the youth still cared and wanted to know the history and remember. The new graves and markers were a sign of respect, and of honesty and truth, he said, and some of the people on the chairs clapped their hands. He said that what was important most of all was showing that the bones and names and terrible stories really did exist. He said that he was proud and that everyone who had gone to the forest should be proud as well, and the almost daughter had gone to the forest and she had hammered and painted and built the house for the candle.

And with this new level of commitment, especially from our younger activists, he said. We do feel that it is realistic to make progress on the museum and the monument.

He bowed and moved aside on the raised ledge stage, and a woman who was older and in two knitted cardigans replaced him in front of the painted head and body. The painted wheat above the painted shoulder arced out from the shoulder of the real woman.

The woman said that while she could not spend nights in tents and dig with tools any more, she was honoured to be working with the new volunteers at the site that was going to become the museum. She said that it was something she had dreamed of for years and had almost had to give up any hope for.

And now, she said. Just look.

The photographs were passed from the front to the back, and the almost daughter did not get to hold them for long. While they were passed, the woman described the exhibition parts that were planned for the barracks, and the washrooms and the administration block. And the guard towers and the punishment cells, said the woman, and the almost daughter heard and saw and also saw inside herself the sand for the long jump and the chalked-in lines on grass for the lanes of the sprinting races. When the photographs and also the blueprints

168

were in her hands, the sports field just outside the town for the athletics competitions stared back at her. She had cheered there and looked at her watch every year and waited for the races to end. It was precisely as it had always been, except that she could see the towers and the remains of the barracks at the edge of the field, and the wire in curls above sections of wall. She saw them and she passed the photographs back.

Someone was asking if official permission had actually been given for the museum at the site. The woman in the two knitted cardigans had collected the photographs and floorplans again. She looked sideways at the man with the broken briefcase.

Permission has not been given, she said. But permission has not been denied to us either.

It hasn't been denied so far, you mean, said the woman who had asked the question.

We have not received any official ban or warning on our actions, said the woman in the two knitted cardigans, and a man who was close to the almost daughter repeated what she had said and added: Yet.

The man with the broken briefcase and glasses stood again with the mural behind him. He was now in the place of a painted farm worker who was holding a rake and a hoe in the air. He said the work on the monument was also continuing.

It is more difficult to provide detailed updates here, he said. You'll understand that with the machinery and expertise we require for this work, we need contacts in certain industries who may not wish to be identified. But I can assure you we are making good progress.

He looked towards two men at the right side of the room, and seemed to signal something twitch-quick at them. The almost daughter could not see the front of the faces of the men

169

to know what they did back. The matt bald head of one of the men was like the shell of a chicken egg, and like someone her father had used to work with. He either had worked with him or still did.

There were more questions and then the man with broken glasses said he wanted to say three things to close.

I want to thank you all again, he said. What we and you are doing is absolutely crucial, and I am confident we will make a difference. These are histories that need to be told and they will be.

He held up two fingers close to his chest.

Secondly, he said. We do need more. We need more of these histories, and we need everything you have. Ask the questions you need to ask and bring us the stories to keep and remember. Don't let anyone be forgotten.

He was saying that no one should be lost and forgotten, and the almost daughter still had burnt matches in her pockets. She had burnt dry matchsticks in her pockets and needed to buy a new box, again.

But finally, he said. We must also be careful. We need to be as vigilant as possible. It is true that we do not precisely have permission, as we have already said, but we do not have an official ban and this is the way we wish to keep it.

He glanced at the woman in the two knitted cardigans, and looked across the chairs slowly and intently. He paused and at first he seemed to be pausing at the almost daughter for several seconds, until this was only the usual sense that someone was looking at or blaming or judging her. He was more clearly pausing at the man in front, who had been the one who before had said: Yet.

170

There are rumours that some of you will already— Or, said the man with the broken glasses. Or let's just all be careful, he said. Let's watch who we speak to, and where, and when, and please do report back on anything you hear. About—

He stopped again and the woman in the two knitted cardigans spoke for him instead. About any destructive or rival actions, she said, and the painted wheat was golden above her. We know what has happened to projects elsewhere, she said.

The man with the broken glasses pressed his hands together and could have been praying. But overall, thank you, he said again. We are making good progress, and your efforts are essential.

He looked across the rows once more, and so did the woman next to him. They were proud in their eyes, and anxious, and scared, and these were the colours meshed together in brushstrokes.

Portrait #37
Portrait in cogs

Outside, another complicating thing. Oksana and Lavrentiy were there, and this part was not strictly unexpected, as the almost daughter was the one who had waited to see when they would stand and leave their row, and waited while they spoke to the man with broken glasses. The man clapped them both on the back like friends or brothers, and the almost daughter had waited and then followed.

The complex part was that where they had gone to was the back of the Palace of Creativity and Youth, and now they were sitting on the ellipsis machine. They were sitting, each on one of the long, flat pedals, where Valya could have been or Elda could have been, and had been only two days before. They were sitting and not pushing and pulling the levers.

Hi, the almost daughter said, and her voice was both weak water, and too present.

Lavrentiy stood and clapped her on the back like the man inside had clapped his back. He said it was excellent that she had come, and that soon she should come to the museum site, too. But for now, I guess I'll leave you two to it, he said.

Oksana lit a cigarette and nodded with her head to the other flat pedal, where Lavrentiy had been, and Valya had been. Looks like this spot's free, she said.

The almost daughter lowered to the pedal. She faced inward so that her feet and knees were between the two long pedals of the machine, next to Oksana's feet and knees, pointed in her own direction.

Tatiana's an absolute legend, said Oksana. The woman in all the knitwear. She's a babe. She's at the site every single day. She's unstoppable.

The almost daughter moved her legs to be more parallel.

She used to be a teacher, you know, said Oksana. Until they kicked her out. Too risky.

Have you been? said the almost daughter. To the site?

Oksana breathed smoke that held in the between space. She said that of course she had been to the site.

It's the real thing there, she said. It's what works. The forest graves are obviously real as well, but no one's really going to see them there. Just hikers who get lost and the weirdos like us. A real museum at the site is different if it's something people will really see. They'll have to open their tiny fucking eyes.

What about, said the almost daughter. What about the stuff about being careful?

So you'll come, said Oksana. That's obvious. Soon.

The almost daughter felt caught tongue in her mouth.

What did he mean about being careful? she said.

173

It's just rumours, said Oksana. It's fine. I mean, of course, it's better if we don't go too often or say anything stupid to anyone. But it's not like we have to speak in codes.

She said that there was nothing wrong with danger in any case.

Anyway, you're brave, she said. I know that and you know that.

The almost daughter was blank at her. She was just a stretched pedal that other people churned with their feet and legs and bland hands. Or else she was the standing one and was churning and churning and yet ultimately still. She had burnt pieces of matches in her pockets, and also the tube of liquid for eyes that Valya had told her would make her look fresher. The tube was in the left-side pocket, and the pieces of match were loose in both. She was the lift and the knife that still did not know direction. She was not brave and she had too many pockets, and the things that she was brave about stitched new pockets and filled them with just more objects.

There's something else you could be brave about too, said Oksana. It's a separate thing. Or it's kind of separate.

Oksana's knee in the space between the pedals had moved without seeming to make any shift at all. It was close to the almost daughter's knee, and to the pockets of her jeans and coat.

It's a different thing, I guess, said Oksana. The river, if I recall correctly. You promised you'd come and swim and then we couldn't and I just think that's kind of a shame, you know?

The hand came from Oksana and was on the almost daughter's knee in the space. The finger traced a circle there – two circles. One for Swim and one for Shame, and through denim they rushed the electric quiver.

174

The almost daughter stood from the pedal. She was weighted with the pockets and objects and the river where skin had touched water without clothing and objects.

I really have to get back, she said.

Oksana said something about forgetting what she had said, and only the museum being important, and that the almost daughter should still come to the site, and more and more about forgetting, but the ellipsis machine was behind her now, and gone. It was behind and far away, but still, whenever it was properly used, its system was looped together completely. Whenever the pedals were churned to move, the arm levers pushed above them as well, and nothing worked in isolation. Everything was joints and cog-wheels.

Portrait #38
In slime

In the bathroom mirror three hours later, the almost daughter's brother was describing a technique that was from the martial arts club, and was a grip to cut blood flow in fifteen seconds. He was saying that it was lethal and targeted, and also that the club was not a club but in fact was now called a brigade and this was better. He was in the mirror and she was in the mirror, and it was fortunate, maybe more than ever before, that he could not read the reflection of her face. He could not see that she was listening only fractionally, and that much more she was hearing what he had said another night, over the sink and into the glass or into her reflection or her. He had been talking about the pervert singers who had been on the television and had been arrested, for their singing or for something else, and were feminists or fat lesbians or both, and he had spat into the basin as if he was spitting slime and acid bile at their faces.

176

He did not see that she was checking the rail for the sleeping bag, even though it was gone now. He could not see when she was on her bed and using the needle to arrange the beads. He could see her, but not the beads in the bottle caps. She made the pathlines of things that felt shivered and electric and wild magic to feel but also were grimed and were fat and to spit at. She made risk-lines and brave-lines. She made circles and rivers. Black wild beads and indigo, briefly. She made circles and promised, distant rivers that crept until she fell asleep.

Portrait #39
The woman with the cave inside her

There are pieces like jewels on the sill of the window and the woman with the cave inside her is with the pieces and in the pieces. The window looks out to the balcony with its biding and falling, treacherous floor, and the pieces left on the sill are what? The match thing pieces? Is that what they are?

No. Not the match pieces this time. The match crisp-pieces are crossed in the corner of the sill like a shrunken, dry-burnt bonfire, and these new jewel pieces left are smaller. Small like jewels, like punctured jewels. The ghost of the ghost of the ghost of the ghost: she brought them and she left them here. She said that they were things that made bracelets and now they make – she makes – something else.

Little pieces out on the sill and a black one and a green one – like an eye. The green like eyes with an ache within them, shined with reflection from outside the window but not enough to hide the ache. The black left jewel becoming something. The green left jewel becoming something.

178

Black jewel on the blistered sill of the window like eyes that tried to look away. Tried to ignore what some were saying, to forget and see only what was meant to be seen. And easy to do this, for a time, because: black jewel eye has finished school and not with perfect but average marks, and no more painting in a classroom now, and no institute but a trainee setter at a newspaper press and so should be content. Secure and fixed, like lining the letter blocks. Called what? The setting. Typesetting, it was. Lining, arranging, correcting, building words. Blocks build words and words build full lines and lines build stories and stories build – triumph. Triumph of progress, of mines, of railways, of workers proud, of grain, of a nation. But black little jewel eye does not need to see this. Only the setting and fixing, positioning. Each individual brass block of word-build.

Until.

Green jewel left on the sill of the window. The ghost of the ghost of the ghost of the ghost brings bead jewels when she comes, if she comes, along with the matches and sometimes the candles. Beads flecked by the sink and the crusted plates, and on the boards of the floor but most on the sill. In lines like twisted paths or in circles.

And setting the brass blocks of letters for words that are not the words she ever chooses, and the supervisor with the side-combed hair who comes and checks and touches her shoulders. Yes, he says. You work well. Efficient. On her shoulders and back and neck like he does when he walks in the city gardens with her. A good, true man, her father says. A party man. A loyal man.

Another way to stop thinking of green, ached eyes.

Until. Until a little green jewel. Rolls into the ink and stains of the press room, into the brass blocks of solid letters, into everything that is fixed and secure.

179

You, says the black jewel bead.

So this is where you hide, says the green jewel bead. Looking for you everywhere, she says.

Studying now at the institute for literature – poetry, beauty and ache into words – and here for the meetings for the student publications.

Can't believe I've found you, she says. Missed you, she says. At last, she says.

And – how? And – her? And how did she become?

And more. She says more: green jewel eyes say more. She says, when she comes to the room with the press and blocks of brass after the student meetings, the outrageous things that some do say, in whispers. Except that she does not speak in whispers. She says what is said of the starvation on the farms and far villages, and the skeleton children. Bread made half from flour and half tree bark, and horses and cattle left to rot in streets, and even then the farmers are the ones accused of stealing grain from the collective. What happens when they are accused or betrayed, and to those who are left who say these things, even in the whispers or jokes. Class enemies. Saboteurs, and traitors. Green eyes say that the mines and canals and railways and factories and progress and triumph are powered by the bones of the dead. Corpses that line the canals, she says, and raids in the night and arrests and false trials. And not even just the camps and hunger that make bones of them: even firing squads in forests. All the voices who whisper to remember the vanishing, and then are the ones that vanish themselves.

Black bead eyes can say what her father says, what her mother says, what everyone says. When a forest is cut to build something new and great and powerful and perfect, then of course small chips of wood will fly. She can look into green

180

bead eyes and try to say this. Black bead eyes into green ached eyes. My aunt and my uncle, say the green ached eyes. In the night and now no news of them. Smashed their cups and radio and chairs and took them in their dressing gowns. To where? To forest? To bones? No news.

You could help us, say the green jewel eyes into black jewel eyes. You could print it for us.

The woman with the cave inside her remembers, and the three letters that finally came remembered. Three letters after no news either from green and aching eyes stolen too. Three letters drowned in rawed hands and rawed ears and the women who screamed and groaned names in the dark, but they also remembered the ink and the press and secrets touched in a room of brass blocks. The woman with the cave skulled inside her – remembers, and the ghost remembered.

Did her own hands that never were rawed really do this? Never had to be wrapped in bleed-soaked rags to drag and haul and stack dread-logs, and ears never haunted with names in the dark, but her hands stained with ink and arranged new lines. Did they? Did they really do this? Because where did it come from? This bold and this certain—

Of course they did, she says to the ghost with the green jewel eyes in the portrait photograph. Of course, she says to the ghost of the ghost of the ghost of the atrocious ghost.

I would have done anything for her, she says. And for chips of wood. I knew what I was doing.

Like this?

Yes, something.

Something like this.

Would have done anything for her and for good, she says.

To have held a ghost as close as this.

Portrait #40
Strangled / Opportunity

The address was close to where Elda lived. It was cold and it had snowed again, and Valya's legs were bare beneath her long fake coat and inside her boots. The almost daughter's legs were not bare, but the clothes she was wearing, which were Valya's, made her feel bare. The skirt was too short and the top was too pushing. In the lift, the metallic clank-wrench sounds and heaving could have been taking them to Elda's apartment, and the almost daughter could also have stopped at any floor. Until this moment, it had been possible to block-ade what was coming, on its own sealed floor. She had not pressed the button herself because Valya had.

It's still an opportunity, said Valya, and the lift jerked and halted, and she had said this already. Whatever it is, she said. It's one step along to somewhere.

There was no sign on the door and the peephole in it was jammed with something that looked like cork. The man who

182

opened it in a creased leather jacket could have been one of the men who had sat and smoked at the back of the marquee at the shopping centre, but also could have been a different, new man. He frowned and looked at the section of Valya's legs that was not beneath the coat and hidden, and then he nodded and said they should come inside.

It was exactly like Elda's apartment was, with the bathroom and the bedroom on the right-hand side of a hallway space that then became the kitchen. The man who was from the marquee, and from the phone, was in the kitchen part that the hallway became. There was a sink and then missing patches and no fridge, and opposite the sink and in the middle of the space, there was the sofa but no television. There were lights on stands shining onto the sofa like the lights that had been too white in the marquee. The man from the phone was next to the sink with a camera on a tripod in front of him. The sofa was the only clean part of the room, like the lightbulbs were scorching to make it cleaner and making it a different place. The sink had wires inside it, and an ashtray.

It's my melancholy princess of darkness, said the man.

The almost daughter swallowed. Yes, she said.

And your friend, said the man. Yes, you did say that.

The almost daughter did not turn to look at Valya.

We'll start with the princess of darkness, said the man. And just in case you're wondering, don't worry. We'll pay first.

The man who had opened the door held out an envelope that was beige and flat to the almost daughter. He gave a second envelope to Valya, and said that there would be more later. He said: Depending on the feedback we get. You know?

The things that the two men asked her to do were to take off her coat and also her sweater, pull the tight shirt that was

Valya's lower, and sit on the sofa and twist herself. She knew that she was not supposed to sit in any normal way, like a person watching television or hearing it. She thought of magazines and websites and videos, and she sat with one leg in its boot on the seat part, and one on the floor, and leaned forward on her elbow. She made the melancholy face by not doing anything new with her face.

The men said: Exactly. The tragic pout. One of them said: A natural.

In the bathroom, when it was Valya's turn, and exactly where Elda's bathroom was, there was not time or space to cry. The man from the marquee had said that the water did not properly run, and this was true and the tap made strangled sounds. The tiles that remained cemented in the floor were cracked with web lines like lines of beads that did not lead to anywhere. Somewhere, there was the line that linked to believing that this was still a good thing to do, and to being what a woman could be, for anyone who looked at the photographs that came from the camera that was facing the sofa. The brown and retching water cried instead.

Back in the kitchen, it was Valya on the sofa, lying curved and with her hair messed forwards, and with handcuffs in her mouth and a key on one finger, and then with the handcuffs between her legs. The man at the tripod was saying that she was also a natural and more than a natural, and that her attitude was what made the difference. Valya smiled out at the almost daughter and the handcuffs hung from her teeth and she was Valya and also not Valya at all. The almost daughter was brown, filthy water.

And in the lift, her face was in the mirror and Valya's was behind it and there, like her brother's in the bathroom that

184

was not cemented and had all of its tiles. Into the mirror, Valya said that maybe it was not what she had expected, but that clearly this was still a step. These people have connections, she said. She said that it had been fun, as well. Exciting, at least, come on, she said.

Flat in the mirror, a face and a self.

She said that she felt strong, and like a god. This is the portrait of Valya saying this. Don't you? she said. Like a goddess? she said. The almost daughter said: Of course.

Portrait #41
In seams

The messages from Oksana came three evenings after the pouts and contorted poses on the sofa and the handcuffs in Valya's teeth that glinted. This is the portrait of how they came.

The television screen was on but the volume was muted, because the almost daughter's mother was speaking to the woman who was in Bristol in England. There were the preparations for the military parades and the sentences of the almost daughter's mother into the computer microphone, overlapping. She was saying that she did not really think that the size of the parades was a thing that she liked. Or, it is a little okay, she said. Of course, in fact, the war was important. But now it is maybe too much, with the flags, and very many days of parades and events. But to say it is so bad is also too much, she said. It is history that is too complicated for us.

The almost daughter had earphones in her earholes and in her eyeholes was the marching, and the children, and their miniature replica uniforms and medals. The music in the earphones had already finished.

It will be tension, her mother was saying. We want to live a normal life and we do not want tensions and problems, you see. The protesting that they are making against the parading is too much, as well, she said.

The chime sound in the earphones was a message and the name above the message was O.

I've been thinking, said the message.

Anyway, the almost daughter's mother said. Probably protests and more challenge cannot happen. Probably the organisations will be closed.

I'm sorry about what I did, said the next message. If it was too much. If you don't really want.

Probably they will be arrested, said the almost daughter's mother into the computer. They are the same organisations and groups like the same ones I told you before, she said. Do you have the word for liquidation? We have this word. They will liquidate the groups.

The almost daughter closed the messages screen. She opened it again with a different finger. You can really forget what I did, said the message. Forget that, but we do still need you for the project.

The same groups that are wanting to find too much history, said the almost daughter's mother. I told you.

I can see you've read this, said the message.

The almost daughter's mother shook her head. They say rights and justice and we need to know about crimes and repressions in the past times and now, she said. But it is dangers. It is problems only.

Hello? said the message on the phone. Hello?

It did not make the bell-chime sound because the almost daughter's finger had switched it off. Chafing and prising the nail of her thumb until it stung and slightly bled was a way to turn things into liquid too, with or without a word for it.

What else, in this fracture of a portrait?

One: Waiting for a morning when her brother said that he was tired and his throat was hurting. She had not been walking with him to the school and past the Palace of Creativity and Youth since the day she had put her hand on Yevgeniy's upper arm in his coat on the tram. Her brother said his throat felt lacerated, and he stayed in bed and she walked to the Palace.

Yevgeniy was at the steps with his eyes down, and when he looked up, he moved his hair through his hat. He rubbed the dull space above his lip.

Hi, he said. I mean, hello.

Hi, said the almost daughter. And hello.

Yevgeniy said that this was funny, and they walked and he did not ask about her brother. He walked close to her and told her how his strength was improving. He said, like her brother had said, that the martial arts club was now a brigade. She asked to feel his muscles again, and he let her and she smelled the sweat in her throat. She allowed her hair to fall over her face and pushed her hips like they had been in the photos on the sofa.

Two: To Valya and Elda, in the classroom, she said again that Yevgeniy had been speaking to her. She told them that he had a friend with a brother who would let them stay in his apartment one weekend. It would be for a night and they would be alone. Elda said that Yevgeniy was tall. Valya said that he was,

but not that tall. Making waves again, though, she said. We'll
need to keep an eye on you. They did not joke like they had
about the cows and the carrots.

Three: There were no more messages from Oksana. Instead
there was Lavrentiy in the bathroom. The bathroom was the
one on the second floor and definitely it was marked for girls.
The almost daughter came out of the cubicle and Lavrentiy
was on the ledge with the sinks.

I don't really think you're meant to be here, she said.

Lavrentiy smiled and slanted his head, and said that this
could be debated for days. But I'm guessing you want to make
this quick, he said.

The almost daughter said that ideally she did.

Okay, he said. So she scared you off and she's sorry and
actually she shouldn't be sorry but that's another story again,
even though it sort of isn't as well.

He touched the earring in his ear.

Whatever, he said. That's for later. It's alright. But we really,
really, really need you. If you're scared of the present that's
fine, for now, but at least you can help us with the past.

He said: This Saturday. In the morning. Be there.

Four: The message from Valya that said: This Saturday night.
They want us back.

Five: Sitting with her father and her notebook for geometry
and her compass. The television was saying that there was
success at the borders and territories to the west. There was
success because there was fighting but not war, and success
because the right people there were happy to be protected

189

and saved. The saved and defended people were patriots, and the good people everywhere else were safer too, now. It was defence and brotherly unity and honour. After the borders were images of preparing for the parades again, and then there were the women who had danced inside a church that was special.

The almost daughter drew a seamless semi-circle with the compass over the paper grid. Wasn't that before? she said. Ages ago.

Her father was watching a football field on his phone as well as the television. He was watching both and not watching both, because this was possible and easy to do. He said it was true that the dancing had been years ago, but now it was their trial or hearing or sentencing, or else they had been arrested again.

It's just another thing to be saved from, he said. More that we're supposed to be grateful for being defended from and kept away from. To remind us.

There was an advert for a perfume in a bottle that was shaped like a gun and had the flag colours on it. It was specially designed and expensive because it was part of the anniversary that the parades and celebrations were for. After the advert, there was the same filmed sequence of the American men who took children from orphanages. The men held their bags that were like women's bags, and were perverted and polluting and infesting the country. The almost daughter's father watched the small white circle of the ball that laced from left to right on green, and the almost daughter drew her circle in pencil.

Six: The portrait of a mask on a face. The mask was made of cream that smelled of artificial lavender, and so was not a mask that was solid. Its name was still a mask: it was a face mask for beauty. Valya had said that it would make her skin and Elda's skin and the almost daughter's skin be glowing and fresh and young and sexual. She had said the same about the other creams before, but this one was better because it had cost more. The almost daughter knew that Valya had seen the photographs from the sofa with the handcuffs hanging down from her teeth, and had decided that her skin was too dry.

The face beneath the mask that was Valya waited for Elda to go to the bathroom to wash off the cream that had dripped on her sweater. Perfect timing for our next performance, she said.

The almost daughter nodded the mask.

A bead for Lavrentiy, or not just Lavrentiy: This Saturday. In the morning. Be there. A bead for Valya: This Saturday night. Beads like serpents. Beads like paths.

Portrait #42
The woman with the cave inside her

The woman with the cave inside her has worn her masks for so long, she knows, that her skin forgets where it might begin. What is her skin? It is a hideous disguise. A false cloak smeared across the years, and yes, a defence, but a strangling also. She has lived like this and her skin has become this. Buried in this veil of years. When the ghost of the ghost of the ghost of the ghost says Mask to her, she knows her masks.

She knows the mask over black bead eyes to say at first that she will not print the words and lines the green eyes want. No one will know, say the green pleading eyes, and they beg into the eyes in the mask and she knows that someone could easily know. The machinist who rearranged brass block letters just to make jokes and harmless rhymes in the names and in the printed speeches; the rumours of the one who wrote the column about the canals and said that there were corpses, too. One day they were here and the next they were gone.

All the more reason, say the green pleading eyes.

So the mask over black bead eyes instead when the supervisor with the side-combed hair comes down to the room of ink to check. Not quite so efficient these days, he says. Something maybe to distract you, he says, and her breath stop-stifles and her ink fingers shake. The papers for the students have been collected already but he knows. He knows. He has seen it through her. But – Something on your mind to distract you, he says. He says he can tell what it is that distracts her and he thinks of her every hour as well. Hands on her shoulders and neck and her back, and a mask to stamp over it all. Yes, she says.

The woman with the cave inside her knows this about the weight of masks. Keep it somewhere outside of her.

Only no mask when the green jewel eyes come. I knew, say the green aching eyes into black. In school, too, I knew. Come here, she says.

So out from – where? The brave and the knowing. Comes from where and becomes what – us? Mask over deepest fathom-sunk secrets and sail to surface only when – with —

Pure swim-rush. Then, the worst of masks. The heaviest mask over eyes when for seven days she does not come to the press room. Seven days? Or nine? Too many. She does not come and the printed papers, the dangerous lines are waiting for her, under the mask of reams of fresh paper. Supposed to have come to collect them and stay, and maybe touch, and maybe hold, but she has not come and breath stops again. Stops and tight and blocked in a throat. Where and she? Why has she not come?

The woman with the cave inside her and the mask when the editors' chief calls the meeting. For everyone – even

193

typesetter trainees. Enemy elements caught and torn out, he says. Weeds torn out who tried to contaminate. The group of students from the institute who came and spread their lies and sabotage. No more of this. Torn out and arrested.

Blink-mask over tears in black bead eyes. Mask over wound. Mask over ache. Mask over the terror of the guessing: at night? Smashed door and smashed radio and shouting? Or silence? In the black crept car to a first dank cell, and lurching wails of names already? This was what the green eyes said herself could happen and here it was. And then to where? The weeds to where?

Masks and all the masks she wore in the years to come and over a life. Wear them to leave your ghosts behind but all you do is trap them with you.

You can't live in them forever, she says to the ghost of the ghost of the ghost of the ghost. You have to find a way, she says.

The ghost of the ghost of the ghost of the ghost holds the envelope. Letters out of a ghost. And out of photograph eyes. Remember me.

What else?

Remember me, says the letter.

Part V

Part V

Portrait #43
Do not build it by the sea where I was born (my last ties with that sea have been severed)

This is the portrait of the athletics field outside the town, which was still the athletics field outside the town, except for the searing differences. This time, the almost daughter was not expected to cheer for anyone in races, and was not in a high-up bus from the school. She was in the same van that had rattled to the woods, though the journey had been shorter than the one to the woods. There was less time to be even partly ready. She was next to Lavrentiy inside the van and there would be no racing and no heavy discs and no metal weights like cannonballs. The heaviest things were other things, lead and caverned in her chest.

Where the van stopped was across the field from where the buses had parked in rows for the athletics. It was closer to the older buildings and the fencing, and further from the seating for the teachers and small stands. The van was closer to the older, low buildings, but this alone did not explain why the almost daughter had not seen them before. They were visible, surely, from the stands and seating.

Lavrentiy pushed her down from the van. Welcome to what's left that wasn't knocked down for brainless laps round a track, he said.

The almost daughter walked with Lavrentiy and the others who had come in the van to the fencing and walls that should have been visible. They were incomplete and broken in parts, but also very much intact in parts. There was wooden fencing in planks on the outside, and a stone wall next with wire at the top. There were two of the stone walls, and then after those, plus the wooden planks outside, was another layer that was only wire. The wire had knots and spines coiling out from it, and this was the section that was most complete.

The turret part that Lavrentiy said was a guard tower as he led her past it was definitely, inexplicably visible. The others that were the same, further down, were just as clear and obvious, even if some did not have full roofs and full ladders leading up to them.

Lavrentiy's arm pulled the almost daughter past the brick building that had two floors and that he said was the administration building, and would be where they would come later on. He took her to one of the low buildings of wood, and said that this was where she was needed.

For clearing, he said. This one's still full of rubble.

He said that others had been cleared already. He said that she might need a shovel.

The almost daughter did need a shovel in the building that was long and low, and she needed the plastic black sack she was given by the man who came when Lavrentiy disappeared. She needed the pointed tool he gave her as well, because weeds had grown out through the floor of the building. The plants had grown into cracks between the frames that were along the sides of the building and also in a line through the middle. The plants had made the cracks even larger and they were also clinging in clusters on the walls. The frames of wood were bunk frames. They had been beds.

The almost daughter wrapped her hands around the stems and stalks and leaf parts and pulled. The weed plants did not want to be pulled but they could be pulled and were pulled by her. She copied the man and then she used the brush that was made of branches to sweep the rubble, and rubble was the word the man had used for the litter and metal pieces and torn beams, and also wrappers and other things that might have been rubbish from the athletics and races, and were left by the students from the schools, like her.

The man said that some of the items that were not new rubbish in the rubble should be kept, and these were for the white bag with yellow ties instead. For the exhibition and displays, he said. Maybe. Tatiana can decide if they're for the displays. And nails we can keep for repairs and restoring if we flatten them out again. They're authentic.

He said that the bunks were close together and in layers stacked on top of each other because more and more people had been sent to the building, and also to the whole of the site, when it had been built at first for not so many. But who knows, he said. I don't know. If it's better to have too much company or none.

He said that in other buildings there were cells that were for isolation for one person only, and these were small and stark and relentless. He said that the buildings with the tiers of shelf-bunks were the part of the camp that was the strict regime section, and the isolation cells were the special regime section, which was stricter and worse than the strict regime section. This place, he said. Can you imagine?

He said this and when he went to get tea, for himself and for the almost daughter, she was alone and sat on one of the frames that had been a bunk and had been a bed, for one person or more than one. There were two women on a ladder propped outside the building who were mending or removing things from the roof. The roof was broken holes and the women could see down and inside the building onto the bunk frames, and the almost daughter bent away her face.

The man, when he came back with the flask, asked if she had come to the site before. She was tugging and wrenching on a root that was too buried. She said that she had not been before. The root was extremely stuck in the wood.

She had filled three black thick sacks of weeds and brick parts and wrappers and unneeded things when Lavrentiy came to find her again. She also had one white bag that was not full but contained the things that the man had said might be needed and important to keep.

Bring the bag, said Lavrentiy. The white one.

He said that they would take it to Tatiana, who would be able to tell if the items were useful. He took a rolled cigarette from the man and tapped on the ladder that the women were standing on.

Where they began to walk was towards the building that had two floors and was not low. It was brick and plaster and it was tall, like the towers in the fencing that had not collapsed, except that it was not quite as tall as the towers. They were watchtowers because of the people who had been up inside them and watching from them, but now the towers themselves were watching. It was difficult to hear what Lavrentiy was saying because of being so watched by the towers.

They were still passing more of the lower buildings and then there was a space between them. Lavrentiy said something that was swallowed by the towers. It was something about the ground beneath and paying attention and something else, and the almost daughter's foot hit nothing. She was falling and Lavrentiy caught her sleeve.

Yes, he said. We really need to tape them off, or mark them.

The square of openness that her foot had slipped into showed down to a cut-out pit in the earth. Lavrentiy said: Tiger cages, and he said: For exercise and the pleasure of daylight.

The almost daughter looked at the low buildings that were ahead after the cuts in the ground. They were different from the barracks behind and the difference was that they did not have windows.

For the special regime? said the almost daughter.

We've got time, said Lavrentiy. If you do want to see.

There was wanting to see and there was needing to see. There was just the seeing itself, and the cold. The corridor, between doors with thick leering bolts where doors were still remaining and attached, and the tight cells with only rotted planks and no bunk frames: this was what was cold to see and the only light was from the roof decay.

When Lavrentiy said that there was not so much time now, he had possibly already said this and the almost daughter had not heard. She had not heard because of the watching tall towers, and the isolation cells and the pits. She had not heard because of the photographs at the end of the corridor of bolted doors, which were of trees that were felled onto rafts and of machinery, and of the haggard, greyed people hauling the logs. She had not heard because of the words that were in quotation marks printed next to the photographs, from a man who had been shot in the knees for begging for a different log quota for his wife. His wife was sick in her lungs and could not haul the logs like the others could. Lavrentiy said that Tatiana would be waiting now, and the almost daughter finally heard through the kneecaps and photographs of bent, bandaged hands. She heard through boned arms and knuckles and followed him.

At the building with two floors, Lavrentiy said that this was where the camp administration had been, and was where the senior guards had slept, and where visiting officials would come from the town and also from the bigger cities. There was carpeting inside the building, and plaster on the walls and fixtures for lighting.

There was mould in the carpeting and the smell was of dank, but there were windows and in the entrance hall section there were picture frames above the windows. The frames were high and near the ceiling and empty, and Lavrentiy said that someone had thought it would be better to take the portraits out. He said that someone else's idea was to mount them in their frames again, to remind people who had given the orders and been in charge, if this was going to be a serious museum. He said that there was still an argument about this, and then the woman in the two cardigans who had been at the meeting at the Palace was there. She had two knitted cardigans again, and one of them was the same and one was different.

A new face? she said. A fresh new face?

202

The almost daughter did not feel fresh in her face.

Not completely new at all, said Lavrentiy, and he said things about the woods and the grave poles, and the woman said that this was superb.

I'm not so keen on the camping part now, she said. But as you've seen, there's plenty to do here too.

Lavrentiy told the woman that the almost daughter had been helping to clear one of the barracks buildings, and he handed the white plastic bag to her. The woman in the two knitted cardigans took a fork that was bent from the bag and nodded. The woman said that the fork was genuine. The pendant from the bag was genuine too, and its clasp was split and the photographs inside it were paled to a milky, phantom shine.

The woman closed the pendant and said that there was at least one more thing the almost daughter should see. Come, she said. Because this is the heart. If people are going to really understand.

The room was where ceremonies and visits had been held and the floor was tiled into patterns, and smooth. There were columns at the walls that did not need to be there, and as well as the columns, there were cut silhouettes. The silhouettes were shaped like people standing, and were wood that was painted dark and black. They were people standing along the walls, and standing together over the tiles, like a crowd without faces and without their voices. Their stories were written in chalk on the black. There were steel workers, and a stamp collector, and the peasants and farmers who had had too much land, and university professors and judges, and students who had printed things, and men who were too foreign, and women, and a priest, and a poet, and a puppet-maker. There was a woman whose one cow had been confiscated and taken to the collective farm, and she went to milk it and brought back one pail for her children and was sentenced to twenty years. There were five years, ten, twenty, no correspondence. This was the *anti-state agitation* and *counter-revolutionary activity*, in milk and stamps and unfulfilled quotas. In *subversive writing, dangerous minorities, the socially harmful, enemies of the people.* More poets, and a student who had gouged out the eyes of party leaders in a conference paper. A mother who had said that the railways in other countries were sometimes better, and a grandfather with the wrong kind of books. The almost daughter stood still at each silhouette, and her shadow crept to fill the outlines. She read every chalk story of deportations, fear, arrests, disease, exhaustion, firing squads, tuberculosis, starvation and lost bones and bodies in the room.

It's a lot, said the woman in the cardigans, when the almost daughter had left the room. She had been alone with the silhouettes and did not know how long she had been with them. I know it's a lot, said the woman in the cardigans. She said Lavrentiy was waiting in the van for her.

One question, said the woman, and the almost daughter had reached the high-up empty frames.

Do you think we should put them back in, so it's clear? she said.

The almost daughter looked at the blank of the frames.

Yes, she said. They should be there.

Tatiana in the two knitted cardigans said that she could come back any time.

She crossed the field. She climbed into the van.

She was late for the photographs in the dirty apartment. She had grit from the barracks underneath her nails. She sat on the sofa and lay on the sofa and held up the objects from the cardboard box, in her fingers and teeth and on her tongue. She arched her neck and stared straight at the camera, except that she was not quick enough. Everything was at a delay and a distance, and the man asked if she was actually listening. Valya mouthed at her from behind the man, and what she mouthed was: What the fuck is up with you? She had the grit deep in all of her nails and the chalk and silhouette deaths were in her eyes. The man said she needed to wake herself up, but she was still his melancholy, tragic doll.

Portrait #44
The woman with the cave inside her

There is a way to stand at this windowsill and watch and not at all be looking out through glass. When it rains. Most of all, when it rains. This is what there is to do and what the woman with the cave inside her does. There is nothing there that is for her beyond the glass. There are only the rivers of rain across the pane, snaked and led by the drops that land. She follows their traces. They weave and falter. There is a way to stand and watch and see them carry away to nothing, and beyond, it can be night or day or dusk or storm or silence or sunglaze or frost, and all she sees are seeping paths. Where they start and how they fade, and fall from where and how they leave us.

One drop that hits and smooths its tail trail is quiet, is dark, is nothing new or special. The same as any other path. And then a drop that stuns and scatters: forks a route that splices the rest. Jerking, spinning, dodging and away. A drop that glints green and fired and aching. And alone, and finger on glass, never touching. Chase it. No. No way to chase it. The only way is breaking shards, and green jewel drop alone and then – where —

I went, says the ghost of the ghost of the ghost of the ghost, beside her close and watching. I went there, she says with the voice of the ghost and the woman with the cave inside her knows.

The rivulets rayed across the pane and their twice faces. Reflections in the glass together, and the snaking like the tears across them.

I never saw, never held her again, says the woman with the cave inside her. I tried. I tried, and not enough.

Finger on the distant, dense glass-side of chasing.

Portrait #45
Portrait in evenings

There were two weeks that passed that were two wide weeks. A person could be in the split versions of herself, doing things that were right in their versions and the pieces of her did not have to meet. In one version of a piece of a portrait, there was who the almost daughter was at the barracks and with the plastic bags, clearing the rubble and things to dump and saving the things that were part of the stories. There were buttons, an aluminium bowl and a ring. She worked with the man who brought tea and small biscuits, and she climbed the ladder that was held at the bottom by people who she had to trust and did. She pulled weeds and moss from the roof and planks, and in the two-floor building with Tatiana in the cardigans, she arranged the objects that were saved and had stories, and she screwed information boards into the walls.

Once, she knew that Oksana was there, in another room or climbing on a roof, because Lavrentiy told her she was there. She did not go to find Oksana. Once, Lavrentiy asked if she would come to the woods again in the van, to replace the grave marks somewhere else and build a new kind of sign in a tree that would say that the place was a cemetery. He said that Oksana would be there too, and the almost daughter said she could not come because she had to help her aunt with planting in her garden.

She made notices to warn people about the pits that were the tiger cages. She wedged them into the ground that was the ground where the leg that had slipped had been her own. She listened, or she heard, or listened. She heard the others who spoke about the archive, which was half inside Tatiana's apartment and half in someone else's apartment, and on paper as well as on computers for backup in case of sabotage. She heard, sometimes, about the monument in the river. They said that it was difficult but not impossible. It would take time, but one day, they said it would stand. The portraits were back in the frames in the entrance hall, and they watched and she did not know if they heard.

And on some evenings, she went with her notebook and sat at window glass and wrote what she heard.

On other evenings, she pedalled on the stationary bicycle, blankly and only hearing the pedals, and on others she went with Valya and twisted her body into the dirt shapes on the sofa. There were handcuffs again, and roses, and a whip, and she twisted and was filthy water, but it was water she could still flush away, and then she was in the bedroom with her brother and he played the games with explosions on his phone, and nothing was really different at all. He played the games with the waving, detailed guns and then did his practice for his martial arts. He said that there was going to be a kind of performance or a technical display, and he was maybe good enough and maybe not.

She was riddled and her mind was not glued together, and it was difficult but not impossible. Managing not to see Oksana in the hallways was easiest for the four days she was suspended from the school. Avoiding hearing why she was suspended was harder. Then there was one last late snowfall before it melted, and even the grey at the sides of the roads and in between parked cars had gone, and things began to happen on top of each other.

Portrait #46
Soon

The first thing happened in the car that belonged to someone that Yevgeniy's oldest step-cousin knew. The almost daughter remembered her lie to Valya, when she had said that Yevgeniy knew someone with an apartment, and that he would take her to be alone there for a night, and so this of course was her punishment for lying. It was not an apartment and Yevgeniy had said that they only had two hours with the car. He had told her outside the school where to find it, and Valya and Elda had been watching and had heard. Yevgeniy had told the almost daughter to bring warm clothes when she came to the car, because it did have a radio inside it but not heating.

After Yevgeniy had said, in the back of the car, that they would have to stay where it was parked on the pavement, he had explained that this was obviously not because he did not know how to drive, but so that his step-cousin would not get into trouble. He had said that he would have his own license by the summer. He had taken off his jacket and tied boots and his t-shirt, and the almost daughter had taken off her coat and her sweater, and then there had been a mess of mixed clothes in the middle of the seat, between them. Yevgeniy had said that he maybe had not needed to tell her to bring so much, because the lack of heating would soon not be a problem, and he had pushed the pile into the foot space of the seat. The pile of shed fabric and coats was the empty outer layer of the almost daughter, or she was the peeled and shell-stripped version. Yevgeniy had said: So finally, we're alone, and this sounded even more rehearsed than what he had said about the lack of heat.

It was when he pulled his vest over his head, and it snagged at first on his gel, and then stretched off, that he said: This is what you wanted to see. All this time, up close and personal.

He flexed one arm and then the other.

He said: We're doing a display, you know? Soon. For the day with the parades, like a show. But today you get the private display.

His muscles were twitch-waiting and the car was waiting, for the almost daughter to take off her shirt. She was supposed to understand the rules, and to add it to the pile of stripped selves.

For the day with the parades, she said.

It's going to be fucking hot stuff, he said. Just because it's not really military it doesn't mean we can't prove we can fight. We can show who we really are and be proud of it.

The almost daughter was thinking of her brother in the bedroom, and the bathroom, and somehow she was in the car.

And then Yevgeniy said: We've got nothing to be ashamed of. You know there are dicks who want to stop it? To tone it down and act like wimps? Some wimp lame group that thinks

212

it's too much and we need to talk about their wimp things instead. Too much for their traitor wimp minds, is all.

The almost daughter stopped her hand on her collar. It really was cold. Too cold in the car.

They're traitors, said Yevgeniy. They just want to fuck us over. Fuck up our parades completely or make them lame and show what they say is history, or whatever.

Out of Yevgeniy's leaking mouth, and the cold was a cold that was stiffening in her. The face in the mirror bent above the windshield was someone who was far away.

Joke's on them if they really want to know about fucking over, he said. They've been getting away with all the whining about crimes of the past and terror just now, but they need to watch out. They're getting fucked back. Their archive and their wimp museum and the whining.

It's coming soon, he said. We're coming soon.

His muscles flexed and crunched again and he smashed his fist into the driver's seat.

But anyway, he said. About this private display.

He said this and then his fist hands were on her, not as fists but as rummaging, dull claws. And like what? Like being gummed, like pulped meat. His tongue in her mouth was smaller or felt smaller than she had ever forced herself to expect. It was almost possible to ignore, but not quite.

She showered for so long afterwards that her brother asked, through the door, if she had drowned. She let the water beads scald her and numb her.

Portrait #47
Soon

The next thing was Valya in the lift of the building with the dirty apartment and its cameras and objects. This time, there had been a kitten. It had been a miniscule kitten that was like a cartoon, because of its giant eyes and shrunk nose. The almost daughter knew that she should not think of what would happen to the kitten after the photographs. It had had a blue bow so that a scruff of its fur between its ears peaked up like a fountain. Valya had been told to wear a matched blue ribbon in her hair while she was holding the kitten, and to make a face like sugar and purity. The almost daughter had not been given a ribbon.

In the lift, what Valya said first of all was: You do realise it's nearly time now, don't you?

She waited with her lips held closed, and she knew that the almost daughter did not know what it was nearly time for.

The casting, she said. It's literally ten days now.

The almost daughter pictured the month in her head and saw that Valya was right, and said she did know.

You don't, because you're a zombie, said Valya.

The lift had reached the ground floor and hummed, and the almost daughter stepped out to the letterboxes.

I've just been doing stuff with Yevgeniy, she said. She could say this because she had already practised how she would say it to Valya and Elda.

Sure, said Valya. Sure you have.

The almost daughter shrugged. You can ask him, she said.

Valya zipped her coat over the clothes she was wearing on top of the clothes she had worn in the apartment, on the dirty sofa and with the kitten in its bow.

But maybe it's not just him, said Valya. Maybe you're distracted and a zombie and weird because of someone else instead.

The almost daughter leaned against the first set of doors to outside and held them open for Valya. Valya pushed on the second set and let them swing to smack the almost daughter's toe.

We saw you, said Valya. We saw you at school. With the paedophile pervert from your brother's year. We've seen you in the hallways. The feather ring boy pervert.

The almost daughter felt in her face the kitten, and how feeble and wet and shaking it had been. He's just another friend of theirs, she said. He's my brother's friend and Yevgeniy's friend. It was something about their homework he was saying, when my brother was sick and missed some things.

Like fuck he's a friend of your brother's, said Valya. He's not. The only friends he has—

He is, said the almost daughter. They used to be friends at a tennis club.

The only friends he has are the perverts like him, like that mad girl you always stare at, said Valya. That's a fact and you know you know it.

They were close to the stop for the tram, but not there yet. When they were on the tram, the almost daughter knew, they could paint things into the steam in the windows like they always did, or always used to. These were the things to always do. They could paint-write names like Yevgeniy's and others that were the right kind of names to paint into steam.

I did know it was the casting, she said. It's just the nerves about getting chosen or not.

Nerves, said Valya.

Yes, said the almost daughter.

Well, said Valya. If that's really true, you'll like what I'm actually trying to tell you.

The almost daughter asked what it was that Valya was actually trying to tell her.

Valya said that there was a plan, and the plan was to go to the casting and pay the fee, and also pay a small extra fee. The small extra fee would mean that a certain one of the agencies who came would definitely select both Valya and the almost daughter, or at least very close to definitely they would, because the man in the dirty apartment with the kitten had connections with this particular agency. Valya said that it was all about connections.

And the only other thing is some filming we do in exchange for the selection, said Valya.

The filming would still be with the men in the apartment but some of the money that came from the filming, if enough people paid to watch the videos, would go to the agency that chose them as well.

216

It doesn't matter if we don't understand it completely, said Valya. And anyway, it's still just a way in. We've always said that. To get to the real thing.

The almost daughter thought only for three steps that she walked about when and how Valya had heard about this plan. She had heard about it from the man in the apartment before the almost daughter had arrived, with the sugar kitten on his lap or on another day, or she had made the plan herself and had proposed it to the man as he smoked. The almost daughter saw the kitten's pressed face and it turned into Elda's face when she found out, and then it turned into a face like a puddle, trodden in and trampled through.

Come on, said Valya, and the tram was coming. If that won't take your mind off those sick nuts from school, I just don't know what will, she said.

The almost daughter did not paint anything with her fingers into the steam on the window. She saw her face. She did not see her face. The kitten had been loose and scared, but now it might be anything. Instead of being left in the box on its own, or taken wherever it was going to be taken, it could suddenly scratch and shriek and bite and skin. It didn't even have to be the man that it bit into. It could be her – the almost daughter – that it came to attack, just for shock. Something. Something shrieking, and soon.

Portrait #48
The woman with the cave inside her

The ghost of the ghost of the ghost of the ghost, when she stands and speaks by the splittered sill of window. Says: It feels like something bad is coming. The woman with the cave inside her nods into her glass reflection. It always comes. It always comes. Just when you're feeling something forming and building, and your face even almost fits you at last, it always cracks. It always comes.

Portrait #49

Фронтоном чувствовала лоб. / Аполлонический подъём / Музейного фронтона – лбом / Своим

And so this is the portrait of the third thing that happened, six days before the date of the casting. The almost daughter had written down the date in the notebook with the photograph of the model girl at the front, and beneath the date she had written only question marks, and then she had crossed them out again. She had turned them into a messed line of scrawl that was like a snag-thread of colour in beads.

On the afternoon that was six days before the casting, the almost daughter was at the site. She had not tried to find Lavrentiy at the school to ask him when the van would next be going, but she had come to the pharmacy it now sometimes left from, and on one day it had not been there, and on the day six days before the casting, it was. Lavrentiy was not in the van, but the man who brought the tea flask was there. He was the one who pointed out his arm to the new upright sign at the outer fencing, which said most of the word for MUSEUM in tall letters. Only the last of the letters was missing. In the room in the administration building with the silhouettes that stood with their stories, the almost daughter read the newest ones that Tatiana in her cardigans had added in chalk. A woman who had tried to escape and was shot in the front of her skull in the woods. A man whose wife had smuggled out his poems and articles in her digestive system.

She was cutting out maps in one of the cleared wooden barracks buildings when the chaos noise came. She was holding small maps that were printed on paper and had a frame of white around them, and they needed to be cut to remove the white and then to be stuck together on a board to make a bigger, whole map from the pieces. In red pen, on the pieces of map, there were circles to mark out exile settlements, and in black pen there were circles where camps had been. There was green pen to show memorials or monuments, and green was the least used pen by far. For the site where the almost daughter was standing and cutting and piecing the map together now, there was black and there was green together, and even though the ink was already there, she traced it again with the nail of her finger. A monument here. A museum here. A black and green circle-beaded museum—

The chaos sound was vehicles first, and it was too many vehicles and already chaos, because so many vehicles never came at once. It was vehicles and tyres and slammed doors and then ripped shouting. The almost daughter dropped the pair of scissors and she dropped the map she had been trimming again because its edges had not properly fit the next section. It fell and the marks in the coloured ink fell.

Shit, said the boy who had been taking the pieces of map and pasting them together on the board for her.

220

The shouting was coming from the building with the silhouettes and chalked awful stories. Tatiana in the cardigans was in the building and so was the man who brought the tea flask, and so were others and the shouting was chaos.

Hell, said the boy with the glue. Out. Go.

In the space outside the long and low building, others were running and tripping and scooping up again. They were holding scissors and weed-spades and brushes too, or they were dropping them onto the earth as they ran. The girl who had a shaved head and had come to the woods was running with only one shoe on, and she stopped still and crouched in front of where the boy with the paste-glue was running with the almost daughter.

I took it off to stamp a spider, said the shaved girl. I left my shoe in there and I can't—

The almost daughter pulled on the strap of her rucksack. Come on, she said.

Or we could wait, said the girl. I could get my shoe and maybe it's just better to wait and maybe see and not go.

The boy with the glue brush turned and shouted his own voice over the chaos shouting. Forget it, he said. Forget it. Come on!

He ran and the almost daughter ran, scattered, and the girl with the shaved head and open pink rucksack ran, in only one shoe and one wet, smudged sock. They ran and behind them the chaos ramped louder. The almost daughter looked back and the trucks at the administration building were parked at diagonals. The men who were there and doing the yelling were police, or looked like a type of police and had helmets and visors, and wedge-batons and megaphones. The people they were shouting and grabbing at to battle into the trucks were shouting back. Meatface? And who? Tatiana? Who? The almost daughter ran and did not turn any more.

They stumbled until the boy still holding the glue said: Here. It's broken here already somewhere.

In the corner of the fencing and wall they had reached, on the far side from where the athletics field was, the wire and wood and stone layers were still standing, but it was true that the wire was bent so that the knots in it left space, and the planking had one large gap too.

We can talk about the irony later, said the boy, and he held the wiring further apart and the almost daughter and the shaved girl climbed through. One knot that was still too close sprang back and snatched at the almost daughter's wrist. She pitched forwards and pulled up again and the boy was through too, and so was another man who had run.

Bloody Jesus hell, said the man who had joined them.

Just a bit further, in the trees, said the gluing man.

They waited in the trees until there was less shouting and then no more shouting. The almost daughter's wrist was cut at the side and felt like stinging and openness. It was dark and the fences looked worse in the dark, and the watchtowers that were closest to the trees were skeleton insects with too many long legs.

They only want to scare us anyway, said the boy who had been gluing the maps. The girl with the rucksack and her shaved head had said that she did not think she wanted to go back yet. She wanted to wait in the trees for longer and not climb through the fence again. She said she wanted to wait until it was safe. If we just wait until it's safe, she said.

The boy who had been gluing laughed without smiling and said that she would wait a long time.

222

The other man said that there really was no way back except in the vans and the cars that were back through the fences if they had not been smashed. It's not like you can get a bus back from here, he said.

Climbing through the fencing back into the site was slower, and everything was slower, and silent. First the boy with the glue brush said it would be good to go inside the buildings to check on things and save the photographs and artefacts and exhibits, or whatever was left, while they still could. When they came to the administration building, there were splintered black fractures of wood outside it and the chalk words were broken into pieces as well. The silhouettes were headless, and limbless, and both.

No, said the older man. Not now.

He brought the almost daughter to a different van because the van she had arrived in was gone already and had left only panic marks of tyres in the ground. She had arrived so many hours and miles before, and now she sat and people talked on their phones. Tatiana in her cardigans had been taken to be questioned, and others had been bundled somewhere else to be questioned, all to police stations with different numbers, and the man with the broken glasses and briefcase had not been at the site at all but had been beaten in his head outside his apartment. One half of the archive had been raided and confiscated, or the whole of the archive had been taken, or burnt. The watchtowers were stretched and tall, and skeletons, and then they were behind and far. The almost daughter wiped at her wrist and unstripped a plaster that someone had handed her. The plaster would not stick to her. The girl with the rucksack was shaking and quiet, and everyone was quiet, except for the phone calls. There was a last muddied scuff of map that was somehow strayed on the floor of the van and it was useless.

In the lift, she let the doors close on her so that she hung in the space adjacent to the kitchen, where a mother and father and maybe a brother would be. Sometimes there were noises from the lift shaft in the kitchen. There were no noises from the kitchen in the lift. It was late and maybe she could say to the mother, when she left the lift and went into the kitchen, where it was that she had been and why she was bleeding from her wrist. She could tell the father why her socks were so drenched, and why his sleeping bag from under the bed had smelled of fire and sausages. She could say these things beyond the wall and then the mother there would be angry with her, or scared and not say anything, or the father would say what the mother had said to the woman in Bristol in England on the screen, about not digging for things and not fighting the past.

In the kitchen that was real or seemed to be real, her father was reading something on his phone. The almost daughter said that she had stupidly slipped in a puddle and fallen sharp on her wrist. She said that she had stayed late with Valya, and she said: It doesn't really hurt.

Her brother was not in the bedroom. He was at the ugly brigade and kicking and duck-punching and she did not want to think.

It had been night for hours when she turned on her phone. Her brother was back or was still out and awful. She had seventy messages and four calls she had missed, and all of the calls that she had missed were from the number she had saved as O.

224

Are you okay? said one of the messages.

Tell me you're okay.

I know you were there.

Tell me you're fucking okay.

Just please.

She pulled off entirely the unsticking plaster and looked at the cut with its new twist-line like beads, and saw that it was a portrait of a day of wires and of shaking fear and ruin, and then she replied. A portrait of ripping.

Portrait #50
The woman with the cave inside her

The woman with the cave inside her sits alone on a day that no one comes. She can hold the jewels that are beads that are pellets and can sit and wait and no one will come. Beads on the window, too, of the snake rain. Across the pane and the glass of her face, and glass mask of her and waiting only, alone on a day that no one comes. Glass dense as a dream; windows as law. Alone like this when the floor falls. Snatch – plunge.

Portrait #51
И если зажмут мой измученный рот

Portrait of a ripping, and then she replied.

Portrait #52
Spirit

At first, everything at the school was normal. Everything was blaringly, airlessly normal. No one was saying anything about raids or confiscations or arrests. In the hallways, no one cared about these things.

On the day of the physics and mechanics lesson, when the teacher did not come for forty-five minutes, Valya called for the almost daughter and Elda to come and sit at her desk. She told the girl who was supposed to be next to her to move somewhere else and not come back. She had been speaking like this more – all the time, now – since the photographs in the apartment had started.

She had a magazine and on the page that was open, there was a quiz with multiple answers to questions. There was a question about what underwear to choose for a first date with a man, and a question about what to do if you realised there was ink from a pen on your face at the date. Elda chose the answers that Valya chose.

228

At the end of the quiz, on the opposite page, there were five stick drawings of giant heads on bodies. The giant heads were blank except for giant question marks, but beneath the bodies there were long descriptions to fill the heads with their personalities, depending on the answers to the quiz. Valya read out to the almost daughter which personality should hang in her head, and listed adjectives that sounded the same as the other personalities had.

I'm not sure about the ambitious part, said Valya when she had finished the description. She said that her own opinion was that she needed to work on her ambition much more, especially with the casting so soon. The almost daughter felt the question marks in her head press hard against her skull.

It was when the teacher did arrive and said that she had been at a special meeting that the almost daughter stopped drawing with her pen on Valya's magazine. On the page that was after the quiz, the almost daughter had added a top hat to a dog.

The teacher said that the special meeting was to tell the staff about something happening that the students should know about as well. She said that she found it hard to believe that any of them had been involved in anything beyond their noses or their phones, but she wanted to say this all the same. She said that a wave of disruptive and extremist activity had surged in recent weeks, but that now proper action was at last being taken.

It is being dealt with as appropriate, she said, and the almost daughter stared down at the dog.

The teacher said that in any case, what the students really needed to know was that order and respect were now being restored to counter the misguided obsessions. And the day of the parades in other cities was coming, she said, and even if their town had no military display, it would still be a day of celebration and pure pride and there were events that the students could and should attend. Performances of strength and patriotic spirit, and a rally and also an exhibition. The exhibition would be of photographs to give a true and clear and loyal picture of what their town really stood for and was proud of. To end this nonsense for good, she said. It's out of control. It's a kind of infection.

The almost daughter sat still and stared ahead and could not see where the teacher was exactly looking.

You are all encouraged to attend the rally and indeed the exhibition, she said. For pride and spirit and strength, she said, and then she said it was time to get back to work.

Valya spoke from the corner of her mouth as Elda and the almost daughter left and the girl who was assigned to the desk waited to see if she could sit down. We could show them photos to be proud of, said Valya.

The almost daughter caught her eye, and then the eye of the dog in the hat, with the question marks in pressed pen that floated above it.

Portrait #53
The woman with the cave inside her

And chaos police, says the ghost of the ghost of the ghost of the ghost. Or something like police. And vans and grabbing and slam of the batons.

And ripping through the fences and hiding and shaking, says the ghost of the ghost of the ghost of the ghost.

And doomed and limbless and slashed to shreds. And beating and broken jaws and one of them mouth-punched and his fillings cracked out. And no museum at the haunted place and strength and patriotic spirit and display, and where are you, says the ghost of the ghost of the ghost of the ghost. Where are you and where is – and how—

So, says the woman with the cave inside her. So do something. So where are you. Your face.

Portrait #54

*Сколько возможностей вы унесли / И невозможностей
– сколько?*

W here Oksana, eventually, suggested to meet was close to the hockey rink and beside the river. There was a playground on the embankment that looked like the playground behind the almost daughter's building, with the same frame of bars that made triangles in a dome, and the same iron lumps that connected the bars. There was a film that was old that the almost daughter had seen twenty or maybe thirty times, with a man whose street name and address in one city was the same as the address in another city, and he was drunk and arrived in the wrong, other city and went to the street name and address in the dark and the building looked exactly the same, and the key to his apartment in his own far city fit the door of the apartment in the wrong, other city. The bars that made triangles in playgrounds were the same and identical everywhere, and nothing would ever change on its own. The almost daughter was sitting on the wall of the embankment and looking at triangles and looking at river. Shallow in the water were Valya's pursed lips when the almost daughter had said she would not be coming to the training that evening. Deeper in the water were the other shapes that were not so easy to catch and determine.

Valya's face in the water rippled and clotted when Oksana arrived, and was grey and deflated. It clotted because of Oksana's sigh, and because of meeting with people who were perverts, or were friends with perverts, or looked like perverts. They were perverts and also extremist and disruptive, and the bars that made one triangle were the edges of other triangles, as well. Where one shape ended and the next began was a matter of concentration and choosing.

Thanks for coming, the almost daughter said, and they sat on the chipped embankment wall. Oksana only sighed at first, and smoked, and then she spoke to the river.

She said that the museum was not totally fucked, but was certainly seriously close to being fucked. She said that Tatiana had been questioned and fined, and sixteen others had been questioned and fined, and nine of them were still in detention. One had had her phone snapped in half. The man with the broken glasses and briefcase and now with his broken eye socket and jaw had been released but was being followed by a car with black windows whenever he left his apartment. The grave poles in the woods had been removed because they violated the natural landscape. No one had been able to return to the site because it was being guarded by the men who were either police or not quite police, and there were skips at the gates that were stacked and full.

They're gutting it and killing it all, said Oksana.

233

The bars that made the triangles held the headless black silhouettes with their stories in chalk in splintered pieces and fading. The items dug out in the barracks buildings that were important and were part of the stories, tangled with the rubble and garbage. Pans, boot soles, a torn book of poems.

It's a mess, said Oksana. It's a total mess.

There were the poles in the forests in the bars of the dome, and candles in cabins on sticks left unlit. In the river, there was loss and forgetting and murk.

But it's worse, said Oksana. About the museum. They're not even just shutting it right down. They're making a crazy new committee instead to pretend they care about the history and they're saving us from lies and whatever, and they're taking over the museum for themselves.

There was a meeting that the teachers all went to, said the almost daughter.

They're having a rally and some mad exhibition, said Oksana. And then they'll have their museum at our site.

Oksana spoke and looked down from the wall and the water spewed with everything she said. The new committee was called the Glory of History, or the Truth of Glory, or the Victory of Truth, or the Glory of the History of the Victory of Truth, and they would have their museum and their rally and their monument. It always ends like this, said Oksana, and she crumbled cement from the wall to the river.

Portrait #55
The woman with the cave inside her

In triangles, says the ghost of the ghost of the ghost of the ghost, with her ghost voice and eyes. Like a puzzle game we used to have in a book with mazes and crosswords too. You had to count the number of triangles in a drawing where the shapes were overlapping. The only way to get the answer was to see that no triangle was completely alone: they shared their edges and their angles.

Sometimes you have to be the triangle and not just the space left behind, says the woman with the cave inside her.

Portrait #56
Этаж

W hat? said Oksana.

The almost daughter was standing up. She stood on the wall and was higher than the water, and higher than the empty names of a new committee that would lie and forget.

I said that can't just be it, she said.

I don't know, said Oksana. Sometimes—

You said it wasn't fucked, said the almost daughter. You said it was only close to fucked.

Sometimes you just have to stop, said Oksana.

And sometimes you don't, said the almost daughter. Sometimes you have to be, she said.

Portrait #57
Этаж

Valya wrote: Just these last few days left.

Oksana wrote: You're right. I'll keep you posted.

Portrait #58
The woman with the cave inside her

The woman with the cave inside her can sit alone on a day that no one comes. At first, there is no one to come. She can sit on the floorboards with match little pieces, or stand at the window with bead little pieces, or lie in the bed and be draining away. She can edge-fumble out to the balcony and air and be falling already, drifting and down.

She drain-drifts only slightly less on a day when the ghost of the ghost of the ghost of the ghost comes. Sit together. Drift. The ghost of the ghost of the ghost of the ghost says: Maybe we really do have to stop. Maybe we're not strong enough.

She re-patterns beads on the sill of the window and locks them into each other and sighs.

Maybe I'm not strong enough, is what I mean, says the ghost of the ghost of the ghost of the ghost.

Strength is a bead that is green and certain, on the sill of the window where the paint cracks in blisters. Green jewel bead of fierce conviction, courage, that rolled and collided with a black masked bead and lit it from inside and stunned it. And did they – dance? Yes. Once, in the room of ink and brass and secrets and outrageous things, they danced and shone because – what? They could. Touching and dancing and alight. Forget this. Remember this.

Remember because here it is in the letters, says the ghost of the ghost of the ghost of the ghost.

Remember so it must be true. Must have been true once. Must have.

When the letters came, says the ghost of the ghost of the ghost of the ghost. When her letters. What next?

When her letters. Three letters of names wailed at night, of the woman who sang the song from the fields, of the day that the song from the fields came no more, of the special regime cells for broken rules, of the lumped cement on the walls of the cells so that no communication was possible in tapped-out alphabets and codes, of hunger, of bile and gruel. Of bitter-ice temperatures before any coat, of hands rawed, feet rawed, organs rawed inside. Of the guard, of lines, of between lines and under. Of bead of strength drained into fear.

Too late, says the woman with the cave inside her.

Can you hear me? says the ghost of the ghost of the ghost of the atrocious ghost. Calling into the cave. Can you hear?

Too late, says the woman with the cave inside her. Followed the rumours to the wrong kind of prison or the wrong kind of camp or the wrong kind of queue for parcels, visits, trick-last beads of hope. Or: First, the wrong town. Or right town and wrong time. The letters cannot remember this part because the letters stop. What comes next is too late.

Too late, says the woman with the cave inside her. Too late. She was gone again, already.

Green bead ripped away further, further. With the baby? The baby. A child grown by now. New bead. Eyes as jewels of – what? What new colour.

The ghost of the ghost of the ghost of the ghost lines the beads, shifts them with the needle, re-spells. Look. Straight into them or the mirror of the glass. The ghost of the ghost of the ghost of the ghost has the same green eyes as the ghost, so. So.

And did you come for her and did you do it all because of her or because it was right? says the ghost of the ghost of the ghost of the ghost with her eyes and her beads into glass and black. And more questions. How did you both know how to be?

What would the answers be, if she could? If they could. If a green bead lost answer and a black.

The woman with the cave inside her: the photograph in her draining hands. Three letters in her draining hands, and where it comes from. Where it goes. Despair and atrocious love in three letters, and piles of too many beads on the sill in dust and grime and fractured paint.

Portrait #59
To set

S o. This is the portrait of the night before the casting, which
starts as a portrait of the word for casting. On the night
before the casting, Valya was preparing, and Elda was preparing, and there were last things to do, and Valya had explained
which agency was going to be the one with the deal, and the
almost daughter was stuck in the word for casting.

The almost daughter knew that the word was one that
seemed to belong to nothing, but she knew that in fact it was
a word from English.

Its letters typed into her phone at first brought only images
of girls in poses, like Valya, with their hands braced on hips.
They stood in lines or on their own and they held up wipe-
clean boards or paper with their heights in numbers written
on them, and the other ways their bodies had been measured.
From far away, they could have been Valya, or Elda, or herself,
with her own numbers. There were adverts for television and

for music shows, and for precisely the casting that would be the next day, with starbursts and hearts around the words.

She typed the letters in English instead, and clicked to find the meaning of the word. A person could do this: could look for the roots. She knew that the layered roots for the words for Memory and Glory and Truth and History were somewhere in mind-thought, honour-fame-rumour-listening, rightness-authority-law-command, and research-inquire-record-dig-wise-story.

When she typed the letters now in English, she found that Casting came from words that meant throwing. To throw, throw with violence, to fling, and hurl. To throw into a mould, pour into a shape, fix into a form, to harden. And later paths: to assign a role, to communicate widely, to set a cracked bone. All of it was fixing that could not be uncast, in shapes, and roles and positions and bodies. Liquid material set into its last purpose, like only knowing surfaces.

Valya was sending another message. Tomorrow's the day our lives begin, she wrote. Early night and get ready to shine.

Portrait #60
Portraits at

The almost daughter did not get an early night, because her mother was talking into the screen. She went to pour a glass of milk, which Valya had said was not permitted because only plain water and green tea were permitted, and her mother was there and talking into the screen. She was speaking and was not wearing the headphones, and was talking about the exhibition and the rally. She was saying: I don't know, and Maybe, and then she was saying: We leave our hands off, which was something she had said before.

The almost daughter poured more bright milk and could pretend that it was tea or water. Her head was hidden by the door of the fridge.

One thing is strange, her mother was saying. A little. A little bit, it is funny. The name for the exhibition is funny.

She said that the announcements she had seen were for the patriotic rally and exhibition to be at the Palace of Creativity

243

and Entertainment, and there was actually no building with that name in the town. There was a Palace of Creativity and Youth in the town, and a Palace of Creativity and Entertainment in another town. So, in fact, the idea for the exhibition had merely been copied from another town, where there had also been a campaign to uncover the history that had also been shut down. The patriotic and righteous photographs were simply moving from palace to palace.

The woman in Bristol asked in English what the English name of the exhibition would be, and her mother said: Portraits at the Palace of—

She typed and clicked and typed again. She said: Portraits at the Palace of Creativity and Wrecking.

The woman in Bristol laughed and said: Wrecking?

The almost daughter's mother typed. No, she said. Perhaps not Wrecking. Creativity and Entertainment, she said.

The almost daughter chewed on her gums and then she wrote a message to Oksana. She wrote about Creativity and Wrecking.

That's perfect, Oksana wrote back to her. That's exactly what it is.

And you were right, said Oksana. We've got wrecking to do.

Portrait #61
Outer

What woke the almost daughter's brain out of sleep on the morning of the casting was the envelope. She had her envelope of the portfolio photographs, from the marquee in the shopping centre, now beneath the bed and with the beads and bottle caps. She had these and she had resealed the envelope, and she had the other photographs from the dirty apartment on her phone that Valya always sent her, and that she also never looked at. Her furious face was there, in the photographs, and her dominant face, and her melancholy face. All in portraits and there they were, set. Powerful face, and vengeful face, all of the melancholy versions of face, and what the men in the dirty apartment said were the three-quarter angles, and intensity and drastic. Bring your hand towards your face. Bring your hands towards your breasts. And barred arms and stark opened legs and closed eyes. Always, who were they? Who were they not quite?

She was cast in these photographs. She was poured and fixed. There was something that once a poet she had read about at school had said about photographs of faces. He had said that he hated to see photographs of himself. He hated them because they did not show him: he looked at them and did not see truth. The only photograph that he could accept of himself was one that had been taken on the highest floor of a building, or one of its highest floors. The almost daughter could not remember which floor it was. The poet had been running because he was late or because he needed to rush somewhere afterwards, and he was running with his son when he reached the high floor. Were there lifts in buildings at that time? Lifts like shuttles. The son was a child and was in his arms. The photograph that was taken then was of him, the poet, and of his son in his arms, and it did not show the racing and running in actual movement and actual life, and anyone who looked at the photograph later would not know exactly what had happened. But he said that they would still see something of it, held, like the child son who was held in his arms. They would see something of the truth of him because of his running still flushed in his face. He was not fixed in the photograph. He was still running.

She lay back in the bed and clicked away from the melancholy face and the postures and the outerness. In three hours, she would be with Valya, in the queue with the girls from real modelling schools. Back at the same marquees set up in the shopping centre and without the ice queen, and there would be the men at the back, behind the camera, just like there had been before and like there were at the apartment with the sofa. Arms and hands to make leading lines and draw attention to the face. To a body. One of the men would be the one who already had the extra fee and would nod or wink or write something on paper, or would say he wanted the melancholy eyes. And then she would be cast and nothing that was really her would be true in any of their photographs.

She wrote to Valya: I can't. I'm sorry.

Valya typed and cancelled and typed and was like the almost daughter's mother, choosing words. The almost daughter trapped her breath. Valya wrote: Whatever. Elda's coming.

The almost daughter began to type but nothing came and nothing would. What came was a message to Oksana instead. I'm free tonight, she typed. For whatever the plan is. The wrecking plan. I'm ready to wreck.

Portrait #62
The woman with the cave inside her

Is this, says the ghost of the ghost of the ghost of the ghost. Am I. Or I don't know.

You just have to be honest, says the woman with the cave. Inside her. Her cave-face, inside.

And remember me, the cave howls back.

Part VI

Part VI

Portrait #63
To fly / *Young women do not*

It was perfectly possible that there would also be others in the apartment that was rented by Lavrentiy's friend: Oksana had not specified this. There were placards to be made and there was planning to do for where to stand and what to shout, for those who felt that they were able to shout. This was what Oksana had said and it was therefore very, entirely, possible that what would be in the apartment was a general meeting, for the protest that was not a protest. It was not a protest, Oksana had said, because they were not protesting exactly against something, but were calling for the things they wanted, instead. They were calling for the museum, and the monument, and for the archive and the forest graves. They were calling for deepened layers of truth. When Oksana had told the almost daughter where to come, while she should have been at the casting and was not, what Oksana most likely intended was a meeting with all the others who wanted to call for these things.

There was the fact that Oksana had previously said that preparing in larger groups should be avoided, but probably the meeting now was an exception. Probably because there was not much time left. There was the fact that Oksana's actual words in the actual message she had sent had been: To make the placards, or whatever you want. Probably, what she had meant by this extra part was making banners and inventing chants, as an alternative to making placards. She did not mean anything else at all. The almost daughter had seen chants and banners at protests in other cities and towns, not on television but in videos. She had seen the time that someone had strapped a life-size dummy model of the president from a noose that was attached to a lamp post. She had seen the protests against the elections, but these were always other cities. There was a way on signs to make the word for Elections look like the words for You are thieves.

She checked again. The actual message: To make the placards, or whatever you want. It was hard to breathe in the lift to the apartment, but this was because of the smell in the lift, and also because of the silence from Valya. The casting was surely over by now, and the men in the leather and beside the cameras would have winked or nodded and made their decisions. Valya would have signed her name on paper, like she had already practised with loops in her notebook, or someone would have signed their name for her, or however it worked with the proper contract, and Elda would be streaming tears. She would say that the tears were joyful tears. Valya would be seething with the almost daughter for agreeing to the deal and then not even coming, or would only partly even pretend to be seething, and be smug because she was the special one now. Her face would be smug and of course that was all. The lift to Lavrentiy's friend's apartment stopped, and a whole group would be there or only Oksana, and the almost daughter knew like doors scraping open that she honestly did not care what Valya would say. It was strange but the drag of it, just then, was gone.

Oksana was at the end of the corridor and had red and yellow paint across her hands. She had blue paint and more red paint on her neck. The blue paint was a smudge or splash, and the red paint was half a print of her hand.

Good, she said. I need artistic advice here and I need it quick and wise, okay?

She had said I need and not said We need, and she pulled the almost daughter through the door. She said that she could drop her coat on the large and rigid package of something that was standing upright next to the door. There were no other coats draped over the package. It was a transparent plastic pack of dried hay.

Oksana turned back to face the almost daughter. Lavrentiy's art friends have rabbits, she said.

Then she launched at the almost daughter and was hugging her with her body and arms and the red and yellow paint.

Sorry, she said. I'm just glad you got here. We need to get to business. Come on.

The paint that was on the almost daughter's sleeve was a message from Oksana's skin, and there was definitely no one else in the apartment.

There was no one else except for the rabbits, who had a cage in the corner of the main, large room, but sat and huddled outside the cage. They twitched and their eyes blinked fast and black.

Oksana had stiff board for seven placards and three of these were painted already. One said: This is our history too, and its exclamation mark ended in a peace sign. The second said: Our museum is our memory, and the third said: You tried to silence us before, and Oksana was painting a thick red line of paint underneath the words on this one.

First I put: And look what happened then, she said. But I just thought maybe that was getting too obvious.

The almost daughter picked up a brush from the tray of blue, livid paint on the floorboards. It was smaller than the brushes from the woods and the grave poles, and wider than the brush for the glue to stick the maps together at the barracks. She did not know how many times now she had painted herself into portraits of brushes.

Clear and simple is best, said Oksana. To show up on camera, in case there are journalists.

The almost daughter asked Oksana if she really thought that there could be journalists.

On balance, said Oksana. No. It's pretty unlikely, but I guess we can dream. They came when other groups were shut down before and told they were foreign agents and enemy scum, but out here in the middle of nowhere they won't care.

She painted a border around her placard.

Or even if they come, they won't show our signs and just show that we hate the parades or whatever, and hate ourselves and are traitors, she said.

The almost daughter looked at the matted bristles and the way that they felted together and bunched. I don't know what to write, she said.

254

Oksana was recoating her thick red line. You can copy one of these if you really want, she said. But I'm pretty sure you do know what to write.

The almost daughter pushed her finger into a scar in the floorboards that looked like a burn. It was from a cigarette or a candle.

It's hard to write just one thing, she said.

Oksana nodded. I know, she said.

It's hard to choose just a single thing that says everything and properly, said the almost daughter.

Oksana said that this was definitely true.

You can copy one of these, she said again.

I don't want to, said the almost daughter.

Good, said Oksana. That's what I thought.

The almost daughter moved the brush to the placard, and the darker rabbit was suddenly beside her. It trembled its nose and the whiskers from it and everything about it seemed to shiver and was scared, but it was also warm and had come towards her. It was not necessarily scared and was just exactly what it was. The almost daughter painted with the meshed-twisted bristles.

They had the seven placards and one banner and Oksana stacked them as a pyramid and took photographs. In the background there was the sofa-mattress that was dirty in a way that was not like the dirty apartment with the cameras and handcuffs and the men. It was dirty in a way that was messy and lived in, and the blanket on it was beaded at ends that were loose and fraying, and calm to look at. Oksana sent the placards in the photos to Lavrentiy and to someone else, and both of them said they were excellent. Lavrentiy wrote that he had just heard that at the school, they would be asked to sign a letter to promise not to take part in any protests or riots or unauthorised assembly. Oksana said that they would not be asked but made to sign the letters.

Anyway, it means they're afraid, she said. And also, it's a bit late for that now.

When Oksana said she needed to go the bathroom to wash the paint from her arms and face, the almost daughter looked at the messages from Valya. She said that she had told her mother that an agent had seen her in the sports shoes shop and signed her to the agency immediately. She said that it was easier like this. I can't believe you chickened out, she wrote. Or I can, she wrote, in the message after that. She wrote: Paris, Milan, Europe, Tokyo, Singapore, and then: I'm actually kind of busy, so bye.

There was a message from her brother that asked her where she was and what she was doing. And also, what's with Yevgeniy? he wrote.

Yevgeniy had sent her a photograph of his arm and muscle in a mirror with no head. Just in case you miss this, he wrote.

Valya sent a photograph of her neck and wrote: Guess no one's said to you today that your collarbone's divine? Now really bye.

Her mother also asked where she was. Her father asked where she was and why, and she switched off her phone and sat with the rabbits. She touched the beads on the blanket that was rumpled across the sofa-mattress above her.

When Oksana came back in from the bathroom, she had less paint on her hands and arms, but still had paint in her hair and on her cheek. She had paint at the sharp point ends of her hair and it was dry and hardened and more than purple.

256

I got bored, she said. It'll come out sometime.

The almost daughter said it maybe would.

Did you want to wash yours off too? said Oksana.

The almost daughter tried to think only of paint. No, she said. I don't really want to.

Do you want something to eat? said Oksana.

Yes, said the almost daughter.

Do you reckon we can risk eating these? said Oksana. She was holding a carton of frozen small dumplings.

Yes, said the almost daughter.

Oksana boiled the water on the stove and the almost daughter found a knife in a drawer for the carton. She cut into it so that it was rough and open and could not be closed and sealed again.

This is the portrait that is many words and all words. What Oksana spoke about first, when they were eating, was how, when she was still a child, she had used to believe that when she grew up she could become a porcupine. She had decided that she would be a porcupine or else an elk with colossal antlers. And I wanted to be able to sing, she said. A singing elk or an operatic porcupine.

The almost daughter said that once her brother had said that she could grow her own wings if she stood on a tree branch. His method had been to push her and wait. He had told her that she could be an eagle if she tried.

Oksana laughed and speared a dumpling that was still too hard with her fork from the broth. You, dumpling, can be whatever you want to be, she said. You can fly if you just try hard enough.

The almost daughter pointed at the paint on her sleeve. She was talking because it was fun to be talking, and because of

257

making Oksana laugh, and also because of wanting to be talking forever. I used to paint a lot, she said. Or maybe not a lot, but I liked it. For a surprise I painted my father's coat bright orange because I thought it was his favourite colour.

Oksana's hair exploded when she laughed. A surprise, she said. That's brilliant.

The almost daughter wanted her to be always talking too, and she was and she said that she couldn't remember if she especially liked to paint, as a child, but she had drawn herself gruesome tattoos with sharp pens, and had also drawn them onto others at school. And I charged for them, she said. I actually made money.

The almost daughter said that this was genius. You could have been a billionaire, she said. A billionaire hedgehog or a billionaire elk.

Porcupine, said Oksana. Definitely porcupine.

The almost daughter apologised.

It's important, said Oksana. What can I say. Who'd want to be just a regular hedgehog?

The almost daughter peeled at the paint that had become a kind of crust on her knuckle. It was light-raced buzzing and freeform to be talking, but there was somewhere further they could reach and land.

And did you? she said.

Did I what? said Oksana.

Did you become a porcupine? she said.

Oksana speared the hard dumpling again. She held it up to the lamp on the table.

I've never been asked that before, she said.

The almost daughter channelled her eyes on the dumpling and its hardened or cuttable layers and insides.

Why did you come to our school? she said.

Oksana closed her eyes for three seconds. What you mean by that, she said. Is why did I have to leave my old school.

The almost daughter looked down at the broth.

Oksana stretched her arms behind her. It's not what you're guessing, though, she said.

What am I guessing? said the almost daughter.

Let me see, said Oksana. Let me see. Either I tried to bomb the school or I stripped naked and danced in the hallways. Right?

You danced like an elk, said the almost daughter.

Or, said Oksana. I threw egg at someone.

Ten eggs, said the almost daughter.

Oksana was eating the hard dumpling. She chewed it.

Or, she said. You think it's because I said things like I did on the stupid day that was supposedly for women.

The almost daughter waited for Oksana to swallow.

Or I kissed someone I shouldn't have, right in the middle of the tarmac outside, and I licked her face nearly off, said Oksana.

The almost daughter waited for the swallow.

Or I came in wearing a rainbow flag toga and nothing else except boots, said Oksana.

The almost daughter swallowed herself.

Am I right? said Oksana. That's what you're guessing.

One of the rabbits was next to the almost daughter's feet, or something was.

Well, said Oksana. It's kind of a shame because it actually wasn't that in the end. I actually just set one girl's erasers on fire.

Oh, said the almost daughter.

She deserved it, said Oksana. She was a bitch and she stole things from me. And who needs a whole mindless set of erasers shaped like tiny bottles of milk?

259

So that was why you had to leave, said the almost daughter.

Yes, said Oksana.

Oh, said the almost daughter.

But, said Oksana. That was just the final straw thing. Conceivably it had something to do with the other times I've used this paint, as well.

The almost daughter pointed to the crust on her knuckle.

I maybe made a few signs when those students were arrested after the elections, she said. They made videos just calling for other protests and then they were extremists and evil.

Oh, said the almost daughter.

And when that one guy got poisoned, said Oksana. And the other one and the one that got shot.

Okay, said the almost daughter.

You know this is how it is, said Oksana. This isn't just about the past.

The almost daughter looked at the placard that was leaning against the sofa that said: You can't just lock us all up again. The outline of a padlock was above the words.

And yes, I may have also painted a sign about a certain law, said Oksana. The Act for the Purpose of Protecting Children from Information Advocating for a Denial of Traditional Family Values, I believe is its official name.

Oh, said the almost daughter.

Catchy, said Oksana. So succinct.

Yes, said the almost daughter.

If what you want to ask is whether I would have done all those other things as well, with the rainbow togas and the kissing, or whatever, the answer to that is yes, too, said Oksana.

You have paint on your face, said the almost daughter.

Where? said Oksana. Here? You'll have to show me.

I know what you meant about the women's day thing, said the almost daughter. I think I do. I know that's not the whole of what a woman is, or what a woman needs to be whole.

Are you going to help me with the paint? said Oksana.

Sometimes it's like that, said the almost daughter. Like I'm not exactly properly right. I don't feel the things that a girl is meant to feel or that a woman is.

You feel what you feel, said Oksana.

I feel like slime, said the almost daughter.

Or, said Oksana. You're made to feel like slime. What you feel is just what you feel. You don't have to fit the word or the box.

Do you know what casting means? said the almost daughter, except that she did not quite say these words, because of the paint that was liquid again and was rivering and pasting down her face from her eyes, and was not really paint at all.

I'm going to put some music on, said Oksana. Sometimes that helps with taking off the paint.

It helps with the paint? said the almost daughter, even if she was still soaked and crying.

Yes, said Oksana. It's a tried and tested method.

And what Oksana meant by music was dancing, with her arms in the air and striped with paint. She meant dancing with her arms up and singing to the music, and when songs came that she did not know, she invented words and sang them louder. She meant dancing on the table that groaned and knocking the lamp to the floor and still dancing, and pulling the almost daughter up and onto the table and into the music. She meant dancing right inside the music, tight and full and free and blazing, with the painted signs below that said You can't lock every one of us up, and the almost daughter's placard beside it, and all of it entirely music.

261

Portrait #64
The woman with the cave inside her

And into an apartment, with a key. Into any apartment with any kind of key. Into this apartment with this key. The ghost of the ghost of the ghost of the ghost hangs questions in the dank of the air. Questions out and frail in the air. Questions out from the letters and the photograph, and ice in cubes left partial and deep. Did she. Would she. Where she. When. How many possibilities, and how many impossibles, and what was it to long for her, in caves. Could you write letters back to her and did you? What was it to write into void and despair. How did you keep on living and breathing. In a mask on a mask on a mask on a mask. And what was the ache inside the mask? And did you really dance in the room with the ink and was it once that time or were there more. And did you talk about the almostness and the wrongness and how scared were you and how were you brave. How was she brave. Where did she. When. And how did you really find the child.

262

Or did you. Or only the child of the child. And what was it to see the face of the child. And what was it to see my face. And is the worst to never even have the right: to remember her and grieve for her and say that you loved her and missed her and needed her. And why is it we have to lose her, and lose you again and again and again, just for a portrait of strength and pride. The story is the endless, bottomless losing. And what would you do now if you were cast in my body and what would she have done and how. And why did I not listen and what should I have heard. The ghost of the ghost of the ghost of the ghost waits for answers to pare from the air and waits. So I made my placard for you, she says. For you and— There. The names. Both names. Names never painted beside each other. History trapped inside a ghost. Thank you, says the woman with the cave inside her. The light of the new wax candle in the cave, and this placard and: Thank you, she would have said, if she could. Would she? My great-grandmother deserves a museum, says the ghost of the ghost of the ghost of the ghost. And the woman she loved deserves a museum.

Portrait #65
Glass dense as dream

After leaving Oksana and the rabbits and the paint, and after where she had gone after that, the almost daughter walked into the portrait of the kitchen. It was morning, still, and her mother asked where she had been, and her father asked where she had been. She said that she had been with Valya. She said that her phone had lost battery and died. She said that she had only drunk a small bit of something but she had forgotten to text from Valya's phone. She said that she was sorry and said that she was tired.

Later, when she was trying to sleep and was thinking of paint and weave-lines to make, her brother said that he knew that she was lying and had not been with Valya. He knew because there had been a party, and he himself had not bothered to go, but he knew that it had been for Valya. Because of how she's a professional whore now, or something, he said.

He said that Yevgeniy had been at the party and he had told him that she had not been there.

So you're lying straight through your nose again, and it shows, he said.

The almost daughter waited until he was gone. She took out the beads, and she took out her notebook, and she placed them on the bedsheet beside her. For the rest of the day, she had the beads and her notebook, and she was writing, then painting, tracing something, slowly.

Portrait #66
In value

At the school, in the classroom, Valya came in late. Her smirk was dark and her eyes sniggered too. She looked at the almost daughter and past her.

The girl who sat next to the almost daughter asked her if it was really true that Valya was now a supermodel and had been chosen for her expressive eyes and her dominant and spicy presence, at a casting, because this was what she had heard from someone else.

And her melancholy face, said the almost daughter.

Yes, said the girl. That's what people are saying. And she was chosen and everyone else who was chosen were the ones who've been at modelling academies for years.

The almost daughter said that it was true, and Valya was sitting and her chair was propped back. She did not respond to the teacher when she asked why she had come in late, and she flapped her hair to cascade onto the desk. She answered only with her smirk and rolled her eyes at the teacher, and the almost daughter heard someone else ask if it was true that she had already been booked to model French satin bikinis in Paris.

In the canteen, girls from the class and other classes and also from the almost daughter's brother's year sat close to Valya, and some stood and had no space. One girl said that she had always known and another said it was like a true fairy tale. Boys were watching from other tables, and Elda said that she had been told that she had been only just off the selection, and that next time she might be chosen as well. She said this to one girl and then to a second, and both of them nodded and turned back to Valya, and the almost daughter was there in the middle and still everything was happening far away from her. She could see the reflections in the canteen barred windows and the bars had cancelled out her face.

It was afterwards and on the concrete outside that the almost daughter saw Oksana and Lavrentiy, and a boy with oversized staples through his rucksack. Valya was saying that she was going to have another and even bigger party, and it would be on the night of the day of the parades because she had a kind of victory as well. She was saying that her manager from the agency would be there, even though earlier she had said she was not sure if the man was her manager or not, and she was saying that of course she could not invite everyone, but that this was sadly the reality of her life now and in any case she would have more parties, later.

Oksana and Lavrentiy and the boy with them were sitting on the edge of the box that had maybe once been for flowers and plants and now had pressed sand and flat cigarette-ends in it.

Your creep friends, said Valya. They're waiting for you.

The girls who had followed Valya out of class, and were stroking her hair and touching her skin, laughed and said it did look like they were waiting.

Maybe they've been chosen by an agency as well, and they want to tell you the good news, said Valya, and the girls laughed even more, and loudly.

The almost daughter was ready to shrug and say that clearly they were not waiting for her. She had the instincts in her shoulders and her neck trained to shrug and look away, and then to ask Valya to show all her photographs again, like the other girls and Elda had begged her to. She could ask who else would be at the celebration party and who the men and boys there would be, and when Valya would be flying to Europe and what exactly the agency had said about her eyes.

Valya was already opening the envelope of her photographs again, and fanning out the ones from the portfolio and new ones, and saying that it was such an honour to use her body and her womanhood this way, and that she did not want to exaggerate too much but she really felt that she had found the centre or meaning or core purpose of her life.

I'll just see what they want, then, said the almost daughter.

Valya's words about the privilege of discovering the value of herself and her body snapped short. They were these words and words she had said before, about knowing her true femininity and destiny and honouring who she really was and could be. You'll what? she said.

I'll just see, said the almost daughter. Maybe they're having a party too. Maybe it'll clash and I'll need to check my diary.

Valya's mouth was going to say Excuse me? again, and was open, but the almost daughter had already moved.

*

268

Lavrentiy said that the placards were perfect. He said that there were more banners and placards that he had made and that others had made, and they would have to be hidden until the right time. He said that Tatiana had paid her fine and that the man with the broken glasses and nose could walk again with just one crutch, but would not be coming to hold his placard. He said that people were too nervous to come now, after what had happened at the site, and the boy with the staples across his rucksack said they were not just scared because of that. He said that there were more rumours now that paid people would arrive in the town in buses to attack and stop anyone who held up a placard. It's what they always do, he said. He said they were paid in alcohol and cash.

The point is, there won't be a lot of us, said Lavrentiy.

Oksana had not said anything yet, and then she said: Basically, they're going to crush us. Basically, this is a suicide mission.

Her arms had been up and then around the almost daughter when she had danced and been inside the music, and her arms had been flecked and latticed with paint from the placards that night and so many times before. Now her hands were in the slumped box of grit-sand where plants had never grown and never would.

Basically, it's fine if you just want to give us your placard and not come, said Lavrentiy. It's okay. If you don't think you can come, it's fine.

When Oksana looked down at the grey sand and dust, the paint was totally gone from her hair, but when she glanced up only briefly there were pinpoint ticks of red and green.

Of course I'm coming, said the almost daughter, and she wanted to be saying something more about the value of a body and its purpose and meaning, but she was saying it slightly anyway, she hoped. Of course I'm going to be there, she said.

Oksana looked up properly then, and the paint flashed real and so did some of a smile. Lavrentiy said he had just wanted to warn her and make sure she knew the risks of it, and even when he also said that another reason that people were too scared now was that the placards would be needed on the day of the parades, the only thing really to see was the smile. Lavrentiy said: It's their own fault, anyway, for launching their messed-up Glory of History and rally and exhibition the same day, and the almost daughter heard only the smile from Oksana.

When they had walked as far as the river together, they hugged and the smell of Oksana's hair was acrylic and dance and fearlessness. Lavrentiy said he would confirm the plans at the weekend in the days just before the rally, and the almost daughter knew she had forgotten to look back to see if Valya's eyebrows were disgusted or enraged or just confused. She was the one who had said that she was honouring who she really was.

Portrait #67
Daguerreotype / Immortal

T his is the portrait of fifty-seven hours until the start of the parades on the television, and therefore the portrait of sixty hours until the rally at the Palace of Creativity and Youth, and sixty-two hours, approximately, until it would be time to hold up the placards. Lavrentiy had written a message to say again that the placards were only for after the veterans, because the demonstration was not against the veterans. The demonstration was against the absurd new committee that was the Glory of History or the Truth of History, and against the way that the museum had been stolen and against the ridiculous exhibition of portraits. The portraits are a distraction, he had said, and Oksana had said they were more than that. She said that they were a keystone part of the warping narrative of pride and blamelessness. It's image control and it's dangerous, she wrote.

It was sixty-two hours, sixty-one hours, fifty-nine hours now until the placards and the almost daughter had red-bitten nails and she had never bitten them before. Her mother and her brother bit their nails, but she did not. Now, with fifty-nine

271

hours to wait with the placard under the bed, she did. It was sixty-six hours until Valya's bigger party to celebrate her own kind of victory, and Valya had said that the almost daughter could now come, but she could not bring her pervert new friends. It was fifty-eight hours until the placards with the almost daughter's pervert new friends. It was fifty-six and then fifty-five and her pervert new friends wrote: Not long now. Her pervert friend with hair that was black and purple and secretly painted wrote: Not long now.

It was fifty hours and the almost daughter took her notebook and envelope and beads out again.

At forty-four hours until the placards, Lavrentiy wrote that three of his friends had been attacked and punched in their faces at night while coming back from buying kebabs. One thought that it had been the butt of a pistol that had struck his forehead, and he was not sure but in any case, they were now too scared to come with their placards. Lavrenity had also not heard from Meatflea and no one was able to contact him. He wrote: It's beasts we're up against. The almost daughter bit into her index finger. She had the voice of Yevgeniy in part of her head, when he had said that people needed to watch out. She stood up to go to the kitchen for water and kicked her brother's empty jeans on the floor on the way.

Her mother was talking to the woman in Bristol in England and was facing away from her. She was saying the words for military and hardware and immortal and regiment.

She said: Yes, it is coming in three days now. We have our day one day after yours. We have celebration and no work. She explained that the immortal regiment was the name for the people who held up their photographs of the brave ones who had died in the war.

She said: But something is too much dangerous, this year. Something is too big and dangerous and especially here, in our town, is the danger. And now it is danger even more because of the people who do not want the too-much things.

The almost daughter filled the glass and drank, and filled again and drank again. Her mother had only spoken to the woman in Bristol in England two days before. The water was lingering and faint to swallow. It was not normal to be speaking so often. She had spoken to the woman in Bristol in England about the rally and the dangers already.

It is danger but I understand, said her mother. I understand very much who is angry and why they are wanting to go there and shout.

The normal square was on the screen but the almost daughter could not see the woman in Bristol in the square for certain. She was there in Bristol and there on the screen and the connection was just poor and unstable, like it sometimes really was, or her mother was speaking the words in English not to the woman in Bristol at all.

It was forty-three hours and then forty-two.

The last thing in a message from Lavrentiy was that he had also been arrested. He had been taken for questions in a cell, but he had known which article number to state to the police in order not to answer.

Another woman had held her placard about the museum and the memories by herself, early because she was scared of the rally, and had been taken in a van and Lavrentiy had met her, and in the cell he had told her what to say. Lavrentiy had been released but had been photographed. He said that he did not care and would still come.

There really won't be a lot of us, wrote Lavrentiy.

I know, wrote the almost daughter.

We have to prepare for the worst, wrote Oksana.

I know, wrote the almost daughter.

It was thirty-five hours. It was twenty-six hours.

It was seventeen hours and the almost daughter had not slept and would not sleep. She had the beads and the pen and was thinking with the pen. She thought again about the poet and what he had said about portraits and photographs, and what was captured and contained and was not. She thought about another poet and her poem describing an old form of photograph. Daguerreotype was the old form of photograph and was printed onto a silvery plate-sheet, and in the poem the poet was looking at the image. She could see it but she saw her own face as well, reflected back in the surface of the plate. The almost daughter did not sleep. She had the beads and had her pen. On top of layers she made more layers and there were distant faces and there was her face. Oksana wrote that the silhouettes that had stood at the museum and were chalked with their stories had been spotted and were dumped and crooked at a rubbish tip. They had been the silhouette bodies the same size and shape as the almost daughter, and their surfaces were matte but could still hold reflections.

There were hours and she still did not sleep and had the beads and the pen and then her brother was watching. He was saying nothing and then he said that he knew that Valya's huge party was soon, and that was maybe why she was so busy writing letters of congratulations to her.

Unless it's a nice patriotic poster you're making for tomorrow, he said.

He stopped watching her and dropped onto his bed. His martial arts uniform was in the cupboard. He had taken it out and put it away again. He was snoring and he was a steady engine that echoed in all of the other reflections.

Part VII

Part VII

Portrait #68
In May

This is the portrait of a day in May. It is the portrait of a day that was close to exactly two months after the day that was for celebrating women. The women's day had been the one when the almost daughter had found Oksana in the corridor and upside down on the chair. It had been only two months, close to exactly, but the two months had been broad with the outdoor gymnasium, the stationary bicycle, the forest, the graves, the dirty sofa and the handcuffs, the haunted site and the silhouettes with chalk, and the fences. And the painting, and coloured jewels and beads, and paper bags and questions to take with the vegetables. This is the portrait of the almost daughter waking and feeling upside down. She was upside down and not in a chair but in her bed, and she knew that she would never be not upside down and positioned the old way ever again.

She moved the beads and her notebook under the pillow, and she saw that her brother was still in his bed. His eyes were open and then he turned away to the wall.

What about your brigade? she said.

I don't know, he said. I maybe can't be bothered.

He said that he might go later, if he felt like it. His phone on the floor lit up with a call that flared the letters of Yevgeniy's name, and still he faced the wall and did not move.

The television was not turned on, and in the kitchen she found that her mother had boiled porridge. She filled the mug that she had always used as a child, with a crocodile and his accordion on it. She ate and the television was off, and her mother was not there and her father was not there. The televisions she could hear were through the walls and pipes inside the neighbours' apartments, and she could hear the music from the military parades. When she swallowed, her throat lumped to the beat of the drums and she also felt the trumpets or horns down her bones. She knew what the vast square looked like where they marched in the biggest city with the biggest tanks, because this was always the same each year. The same and only her throat was different.

She was pulling on her shoes when her father did come out. He was wearing the shirt he had been wearing in the evening, and his chequered shorts. His legs were narrow and pale and did not march, and she waited for him to switch on the screen. The speeches were beginning, tight through the walls.

He did not lift the remote control from the tabletop. He sat on the sofa and looked at the bare screen, and he had no woman in Bristol in England to pretend to speak to, and so he stood again. He faced her.

278

Just be careful, he said. Just be very, very careful.

He put his hand on her arm and led her zip to her chin. It was something he had used to do when it was cold and she had said she was not cold, and he had said he would wrap her warm like a sausage, even if, now she thought of it, a sausage was not especially wrapped. She nodded and he nodded, too. The placard with both names bold in paint stuck one corner out of her bag.

In the lift, she ran two fingers over the buttons for every floor, for luck, but she knew exactly where she was going.

As she walked, there were many people – so many – walking. There were also buses from the edges of the town or from villages that had been specially arranged, and tickets did not need to be stamped. They were to bring bodies in to join the rally, and she was tucked in the middle of the walking bodies. The placard was easily covered with an extra sweatshirt and could have been a flag on a stick, like the others held up or in bags all around. A slow girl stopped walking and said that she felt sick, and her mother said she was just excited. The girl cried and said there were too many people, and the mother said it made sense to be excited. Some of the roads had been closed to traffic, as if there could be a parade on them as well, with the tanks and the equipment and instruments, but they were closed to be full of the people instead.

The stage was wood and clipped bars of metal in front of the Palace of Creativity and Youth. There were stalls that were selling fried onions and pastries and mustard and more hanging flags and striped ribbons. The almost daughter wanted to eat fried onions for strength, and she nearly bought a plate of them, but did not. She saw the boy who had been called

Meatflea in the crowd, and then he disappeared and the feeling inside her of needing strength from something spread deeper. The onions smelled drenched and delicious but also distant and they would not help. The girls on the stage were dancing in tiaras. The almost daughter had a red tiara like they did, in the cupboard where she had kept the beads and the loom, and a dress like they did, and now it was too small.

After the dancing girls, the veterans replaced them, and sat on tall stools around the edge of the stage. A man who was not the mayor of the town but was one of the men who worked with the mayor pinned medals over the existing medals. The almost daughter clapped with the crowd, because the veterans were not to blame. Lavrentiy had said they were not the ones to blame, and Oksana had said they were not the ones to blame.

Next in the portrait on the stage were the men and boys with black cloth tied around their foreheads, and grey or camouflage trousers and no shirts. The almost daughter's hands stopped clapping because they knew this was the martial arts brigade, and she closed her eyes and opened them and Yevgeniy was there. He kicked sideways and blocked one boy with his fist high, and flicked another boy to the ground, and in front of him the man who was not the mayor said the country was clearly in safe, youthful hands. He said that this was important, for the borders and all the threats, and people cheered. Yevgeniy was there and sweat-shined and shirtless, like he was in one of the photographs he had sent and the almost daughter had not replied to, and she checked again while the crowd cheered more. Each of the faces on the stages, but no. Yevgeniy was there, and her brother was not.

The man who was the actual mayor and had explosive, sprouted eyebrows joined the stage. He walked to the centre and stood next to the deputy, but was not completely next to the deputy because of the two men who also came with him, who were not deputies who worked with him but always pressed on either side of him. They were the giants who protected him and had coil-cords that looped to behind their ears. The mayor smacked his palm on Yevgeniy's back.

Yes, in powered, strong hands, he said.

The almost daughter felt the corner of the placard sticking out from her bag and through the sweatshirt.

And it gives me great pride and pleasure, said the mayor. To make the announcement I know you've all been waiting for. I make it in the name of these youthful, strong hands.

The mayor's mouth moved and the eyebrows did not. He said everything that Oksana and Lavrentiy, and also Yevgeniy, in the parked car, had said. He said that a dangerous and criminal band of traitors had been preparing to launch their strange lies on the town to blacken its image and humiliate its truth.

And not just to humiliate us here, he said. They want to humiliate our whole nation and spirit.

The crowd made waves of muttering and two women who were close to the almost daughter shook their heads. They wanted to make us eat our dirt, said one.

They say they want to recover the memories of the innocent, said the mayor. They say they want a museum for victims. Do they forget how many more innocent lives were sacrificed to the actual enemy? Why do we need to talk about so-called repressions and deform our pride?

The mayor pointed to the veterans behind him and the deputy mayor also pointed and stood straight.

I ask you, said the mayor and his eyebrows. Why should we, the descendants of victory, be ashamed and repent and not take pride in our past?

The almost daughter was ready for her voice. She was clear and ready, but she waited for the sign. Oksana was supposed to shout first. Oksana was somewhere and was meant to be first.

The answer is that we must not be ashamed, said the mayor from his slack face that did not move. We have taken the extremists out of action and we will have our museum of glory instead.

He said that the museum of truth and glory and history would be opened soon. First it would be in the Palace of Creativity and Youth, behind him, and would start the next day with the portraits exhibition. He said that this would show the real pride and real truth and not the lies and denigration.

And then, he said. We will have our monument, to our real heroes, to stand in our river. Our monument will be taller and stronger than ever. And in the third phase we will transfer our museum.

He said that the museum would be transferred to a historical site outside the town, in a new and beautiful, gleaming building. He said that the structures at the site that remained were much too dangerous and much too old and would have to be demolished for safety.

That will be our museum, he said. When we cut the forest to build our great house – yes, there are the woodchips that fly. But look at our house! Look at our house now!

The almost daughter's ears filled with woodchips and with the broken black silhouettes at the site that the mayor was saying

282

would be demolished forever. This was surely the sign now or past the sign, before the cheering and saluting were too loud. Already the cheering was too loud, and nothing. There was no voice of Oksana or Lavrentiy or Meatflea or anyone else who should be shouting and flying the woodchips back into their voices.

The glory of history! called out one of the women who were close and who had shaken their heads. She was looking upwards now, to the stage.

To the glory! called the second woman, who had said that she had been made to eat dirt.

To the glory of history! called more and more, and then it was a rhythm and a pounding. It was the glory of history, and the truth of history, and the glory of truth and a pounding animal. The animal was thumping from the mayor on the stage, and the deputy mayor, and the boys from the brigade, and still there was no one giving the sign. Children were eating milk ice-cream from wrappers. They had the cream all over their faces and dripping onto their miniature uniforms. They had the ice-cream and they had the hot chestnuts, and their hands were sticky with both at the same time, and the pounding of glory was relentless and deafening.

Demolishing, said the almost daughter.

The woman cheering and calling beside her looked at her but had not heard.

You're the ones, said the almost daughter, and she was louder now and the woman was frowning. She was cheering still, and also frowning, and moving away from the almost daughter.

You're the ones deforming our history! called the voice from inside the almost daughter.

And maybe it was the very same moment, or maybe it was only just afterwards, after the almost daughter's voice

283

was loud enough and had been first. Whether it was at the same moment or just after, it came and it was in one place and then it was from more scattered places at once.

It was: Stop the silencing!

It was: Tell our whole story!

It was: Censorship! Tyranny! We are the memories!

It was the placards and banners sudden out of backpacks, and Oksana on Lavrentiy's shoulders and screaming. It was: Shame! It was: Shame! It was: Never forget! It was paint and names and dates on the placards, from the graves in the forest and the black silhouettes. Somehow – there, and there – it was the real silhouettes, rescued from the site of the camp or maybe made again and chalked, and they were up in the air and held high with the placards. It was Oksana now on Meatflea's shoulders, and Shame! and Never forget! and Memory! It was Shame and Never forget and then the boys without their shirts from the brigade – Yevgeniy? – catapulting down into the crowd. The screaming out of Razing our history! You're the ones demolishing our history! and the almost daughter had said it first and down came the boys and their bare-skin chests and the men with the mayor spoke into their coiled wires. Oksana holding tight to the placard that she had painted with her painted hands and all the placards and all the words and the boys from the brigade and then men from the buses parked along the sides of the Palace, forcing through with plastic shields and baton stripes and the visor-helmets – Here! from the woman still close and pointing. There's one right here – one more filthy traitor, and the shields and visors turning, coming, but also the hand on her back and a Thank you and You did this and If you hadn't started. Hands on her back and shoulders and foot on one hip and Oksana trying to climb – to climb and still hold up the placard – Here! They're right here! and the shields pressing closer, and surely not so far away, in the room where there were the photographs of two women so atrociously in love and strong, the words and voices and paint were loud enough and the almost daughter was loud again. It was Demolishing our history! You're the ones! and surely the strong, lost women would hear.

It was Oksana wrenched and clattered from her back. It was the placard for the women and caves snatched and hurled and trampled on fast. Men in the helmets surrounding and dragging and – The other one too! She was here first! and ducking and scrambling and pulling away. Oksana dragged through the animal crowd to the dark glass of buses and turn to her just once. To her? – or the other direction – away. No lungs, no voice now. Abandon: a portrait. Abandoned, trampled, dragged: a portrait.

Portrait #69
The woman with the cave inside her

Can she hear this?
　　What can she hear?
Only hope that she – they – might hear.
Hear voices calling back for them, then cut.

Portrait #70
Photosensitivity

A portrait is a thing that can happen and change. A portrait is a force that is not a sealed surface. It is everything beneath its layers, and is sculpted out from cubed ice blocks, unfinished and inexact and still shaping. Here is what can happen in a portrait, even if you are a person like this: even if you have run away. When you have fled, again, not through wire that shreds, but again away from danger and all kinds of clawing. Because you run towards as well as away, and here is where you run to, in a portrait. In a portrait that sees where you're racing from and where it is you're racing to. Aperture. How we do this; why we do.

Portrait #71
A father, a mother

You run first – run panting stairs and slipped feet – run first to where your father is. You can be here in this apartment and breathless and this happens. Your father alone at the kitchen table, in front of the screen that is not his. Next to him, on a chair, a sleeping bag, out from beneath his bed and pretence.

Hello, he says, and he speaks in English. Hello. I am here with you to make speaking.

His voice to the screen in English is a new voice. Or it is just that the words are so different from him.

Good day, he says. I need to tell you. My wife is not – cannot tell you this thing.

You can be here in this apartment and listen and this happens.

She wants to say that this shouting on this day is the right thing that must come from us, he says. She knows it is the right thing we must do, even if it is hard for us. Even if it brings us this hard pain and this danger.

You can be breathless and hearing this from your father, at last, and from your mother, in the voice of your father.

It is right, he says. Yes. It is hurting us but right. We need the memories to live. We do need.

Portrait #72
And your brother

And your brother. He can say: These are actually good. He looks up from your row-beads and hummed colours in the bedroom, and the words you have lined for them as portraits as well.

Your grown gone brother you used to know and then you thought you knew again. He follows your beads and the words and understands.

And the photograph, he says. She looks like you.

What you've done with it, he says. All of these.

I know who she is, he says. I know. And this one too. I know who she was.

But what are we going to do with them? he says.

He can say: Let's go then. You're ready for this, aren't you?

And your mother can be just through the crack of the door, but she is there and she is also telling you to go. Just be very, very careful, your father can say.

So you go. You take your own woven grown voice with you and in it the two faces you have tried to hear, which are not everything, of course, but are something. Go. Take these scissorblades. Take scissors and tape. Take faces and voices; take and race with your brother.

Portrait #73
In victory

It is you who says to your brother that you should stop at the party first, on the way. He says that it makes no sense to go, and you say that for you it really does. He lets you press the buttons in both lifts, once to go down, and then to go up. One day, maybe, you will tell him why you know this building already. And this floor. Or he has guessed this for himself. It's been hard to know who to be, you'll say, and where to stop and shudder doors open and he'll have to understand, and he will.

Inside the dirty and now body-packed apartment, where the sofa is, and where the handcuffs were, and where the kitten was soft and you feigned yourself, you watch Valya from where she can't see you. She can't see you because of all the crammed mass here, rotating and in pressed and unlikely combinations. Of men in the leather jackets and tight suits, of girls who must be from the school or even younger, of older women who look lank and strained out. What does Valya see?

292

Does she really see Paris? Here, a portrait of glamour, somehow smeared across the poured concrete and sweat? She is leaning by tacked-on cupboard doors and one man is looming towards her on one side and on the other, a man in a shimmering shirt is slumped and his stubble is coarse at her cheek. You can feel how much like sandpaper it is, and constant. Sweetness, he is breathing at her, or: Drive me wild, or Let me just, and then his tongue is the texture wet next on her neck.

And more of Valya, everywhere and looping, because across the bare walls and the bodies and noise there is her face and all her faces, repeated. Images beamed from the beige-grey box projector balanced on the arm of the sofa. Out from somewhere digital and stored, through the hot, clagged air and onto the surfaces: Valya's face and poses and skin. Commanding face, wild innocence face, empowered-unleashed face, *come and get me* face. From the shoot for the first portfolio, from this room and this sofa with the handcuffs and roses, and more you haven't seen before: a peacock feather, a whip, fruit and cream. Face framed in a flag and a military cap – this too now. A portrait, a portrait, a portrait. Tied and melded together by the crystal lights from the black plastic ball that is also balanced, also beaming colour. Spasms of the light in shard-triangle pieces to intersect with Valya's faces and relentless and overlapped like the music. And because of course you can't not think it: Could have been your faces projected, could have been your neck slabbered with tongue now. Blink and it is you. To know how to be.

Retching from the bathroom now and two boys pound and the door opens slow. Opens. Or is this the one that's you? Is it Elda? Door opens and out, sick and keen, another flash of translucent Valya on this face, too. It isn't you. It isn't even Elda.

Just another swept and cast girl-shape, believing or hoping or gagging to believe that she knows how and who she ought to be and moulded to fit the outlines around her. Blink and any of these warps can be you. Beamed out.

Damp hand on your neck then – real neck. Yours. Like this? Why is it always like this?

I knew you'd come, says Yevgeniy to your neck. The alcohol tang and leak stain on his lips. Or the drugs that have the names of reptiles. I knew you'd know what's good for you, he says.

His clam-thick hand. Where else it has been – today? Yes, it is still today. Slammed into voices, silhouettes, placards, paint and hope and woodchips, flown memory. Even now, in a knot nearby, a splat of the boys and also the men mimicking and saying: Victory. Glory. Grandfathers and heroes and pride. This country is finally coming together and standing up and fucking strong in its history, and the traitors want to make it pathetic and guilty.

And your neck. What does Yevgeniy – anyone – see? Can't see if you don't let them see.

What are those scissors for? says Yevgeniy.

You nod to your brother and your brother nods his eyes back. Time to go. Time for you and more faces.

What are you doing with those scissors? says Yevgeniy. You look – you do look a bit mad, if I'm honest.

What you look like. *Young women do not look like this.*

Behind. Leave these flung-beamed false portraits behind now.

Come on, says your brother. Enough.

294

Portrait #74

An exhibition / *See, hear, touch you all*

A face.
A face.
Cut. Cut.
A face.
A face.
A face.
A face.
A face.
Wreck this.
A face.
A face.
A face.
Та – риз моих, та – бус моих
Та – глаз моих, та – слёз моих
A circle.
A face.

A face.
This face.
These eyes.
The face.
A face.
A face.
Two faces.
Again, and cut and let them. Here.

Portrait #75
Out of these meagre, overheard words

A nd then, the woman with the cave inside her, or else the cave with a woman inside it.

Because the woman with the cave raged inside her and out of her and all around her is waiting. And they come – they all come, tonight. The ghost first of all, because always the rawed ghost. Then the ghost of the ghost: the lost child she never met. And the ghost of the ghost of the ghost, and no vegetables. And the ghost of the ghost of the ghost of the ghost, with her notebook and tiny jewels and her eyes. A pair of scissors as well, this time. Flash from metal and from ghost-eyes and jewel beads.

Oh, says the ghost of the ghost of the ghost of the atrocious ghost. What— Why are you—? Why here?

Oh, says the ghost of the ghost of the ghost. I didn't think. Didn't know that you—

They are silent. They watch glass rain in snakes. They watch the still beads on the sill of the window, and the pieces of brittled dry matches and ash.

I still come here, sometimes, even now, and sit, says the ghost of the ghost of the atrocious ghost. Even now she's gone as well. I just come.

I know, says the ghost of the ghost of the ghost of the ghost. Me too. I've been using your key. Since she – since—

I just change her sheets and wash the plates, like before, says the ghost of the ghost of the ghost. It feels like it's something I can do for her and both of them.

I pretend I'm – like I'm speaking to her, says the ghost of the ghost of the ghost of the ghost.

Speaking? says the ghost of the ghost of the ghost.

Listening, says the ghost of the ghost of the ghost of the ghost, and her mother frowns, and then nods.

From her letters, says the ghost of the ghost of the ghost. You found the letters she kept here and read them.

Three letters, says the ghost of the ghost of the ghost of the ghost. And what I heard and just figured out.

She says: printing, typesetting, the secret, the shame, the disappearing, the letters, rawed hands. The marrow-shivering, the cursed days, rot bunks, the groans and names in screams at night.

The guard, says the ghost of the ghost of the ghost.

The child, says the ghost of the ghost of the ghost of the ghost. Then the child of the child, and her child.

We didn't want to know her, says the ghost of the ghost of the ghost. It was too hard. It was safer and easier and more normal to forget.

The cave in her, says the ghost of the ghost of the ghost of the atrocious ghost.

298

Yes, says the ghost of the ghost of the ghost.

Before she fell, says the ghost of the ghost of the ghost of the ghost. Before the balcony fell.

Yes, says the ghost of the ghost of the ghost.

She wanted to remember, says the ghost of the ghost of the ghost of the ghost.

I wanted to, says her mother. At first. And your father did. He tried even more. At first. But then—

Then? says the ghost of the ghost of the ghost of the ghost, and she already knows.

It was like it is now, and too risky, says her mother. He went out to the woods to dig and see as well, and they built the monument to stand in the river. He was part of all that, when I couldn't do it. And then there were the fights because of course they were traitors. It's hard and you know that. You have to know.

And then she fell, says the ghost of the ghost of the ghost of the ghost. She fell and we lost her too.

Yes, says the ghost of the ghost of the ghost.

If we don't remember, says the ghost of the ghost of the ghost of the atrocious ghost, or this is what her thread wants to say. Then I can't know who we are and who I am. I can't know how and who to be.

Candlewax and matches and small woven heart-beads. A writer. Another poet? A writer. *Dwell on the past and you'll lose an eye. Forget the past and you'll lose both eyes.* Jewels for lost eyes at this shrine of a sill.

We'll come here, says the ghost of the ghost of the ghost. We'll remember them both when we come here for them. The letters left and their photographs left.

And they— There's something I've done to remember them, says the ghost of the ghost of the ghost of the ghost.

Good, is what her mother says, or would say.

And there's one more last thing, tomorrow, says the ghost of the ghost of the ghost of the ghost. It's for me and it's for her as well, in a way, and the ghost of the ghost of the ghost holds arms around her and they have this shared candle.

The ghost in this room. *Remember me.* In the ghost of the ghost of the ghost of the ghost. Casts herself, decides her own face-shape.

The woman with the cave inside her, and a flame alight inside the cave, and a flame of ghosts and of the ones that remember. *This wide shroud of words still heard.*

Portrait #76
Девический дагерротип / Души моей

This is her final portrait, for the moment. This is her final and deep-woven portrait. When and where, and full of this last river.

River of Oksana, who arrives before the sun. River of a cell in a basement overnight, and straight to the river when the almost daughter asks. River-portrait of coming straight from a cell and cracked sleep on rigid tiles, and puffed eyerims, and straight to the embankment wall of the river to sit with legs hanging down and limp.

And I have to go back there tonight, says Oksana. To sign in and report so they know I haven't run. For the rest of the week and then I don't really know.

River of smoking and counting through fingers. Lavrentiy sent away from the school forever, Tatiana and some of the others sent further, and maybe for years and the same as forever. Not camps now, of course, she says. Just your average shitball penal colony and beatings and gagging and a way to shut us up before whatever insanity they're cooking up next.

River of a final portrait, for the moment. Face over face over bleak-worn face.

Breach of public assembly procedures, and dangerous extremism, says Oksana. I'm really quite dangerous, in case you hadn't noticed.

River of a sigh and a hope-wracked face.

I'd noticed, says the almost daughter.

Good, says Oksana. At least that's something.

River of saying that at least it was something, and shrugging and breathing smoke from her nose as if its trails can be careless and calm and not afraid, but eyes collapsed at the ugly water.

No one gives the tiniest shit, she says. It hasn't made a rat-speck of difference.

River of legs hanging loose and down, against the almost daughter's legs. Until—

It's dead, says Oksana. Just was never even worth it.

River of worthless, pointless, depleted, and thick and dismal and stifling water. Until—

Stone of the embankment wall cold – on skin. Opposite – triangle bars in the playground, scabbed in the dome of last shapes and framing.

What are you doing? says Oksana in smoke.

River of unlacing a second shoe and peeling away a second sock. Both feet now cold on the barrier wall. Stands – stands legs tall and unhooks her jeans.

Just taking off my scarf, she says, and she pulls off her sweater and her shirt in its sleeves—

—because river here and she is going to jump. She will hit the water purely and burst spirals, and Oksana will hit, if she

302

flies with her too – she will take and lead Oksana's hands to the tips of a monument still covered and choked, but there and waiting and for the victims of true terror. River of whatever shape the monument was once and whatever shape they can make it be, and the tips of it and the whole of it, and bring Oksana's hand, if she jumps too, to the texture of it and all water – all ice. If Oksana will jump before she has to go, and wherever she is taken now or sent, and however long she, the almost daughter, will be alone for without purple riot hair again, and cave-lost and needing but knowing and feeling – if Oksana jumps now, she can show her it was worth it. She can show her through water – churned water and river – all the false portraits she and her brother saw for the lying exhibition in the night: portraits of smiles, couples, the mayor, crisp-brash flowers cupped next to faces, the brigade and the winter sculptures out of ice. Holding flags and draped in flags, and poses like Valya's and gleaming teeth, and all of it only the town at its surface – no haunted fields, no forest, no hulk towers, no tiger cage holes hollowed dead beneath, no sleep slashed through with howling names, no songs that bled and disappeared. No *clamped-shut and tormented mouth through which the hundred million scream*, no cave gouged always of love and loss – no *Remember—*

And then she can show – and then river sting can show—

Jump and crash and brace colder and piercing—

Crash and if Oksana will just leap now as well—

If she flies and when she flies—

Jump and crash and even colder and piercing. Crash, and if Oksana – when – tell her through this water and bone-freeze – what she and her true brother and a pair of quick scissors. Scissors to the lying portraits – to cleave into fakery

303

and gash into masks, and in their place instead with the packing tape that her brother stripped and bit-tore into pieces – the photographs, in her copies of them, of green jewel ache eyes and black jewel cave eyes – and two names beneath them that belong together, finally. And *Remember me* – remember, remembered, and the clamped names at last. And then everything was ready and a monument, and in four hours now the exhibition will be open, and ruined and rip-wrecked and true – good to have known which window to pry and clamber to and scale down from inside – good. No museum – yet – but these true portraits at last—

Water in her mouth. River of her mouth. And I need you in this portrait, she says.

And river of Oksana jumps – flies and crashes. Crushlands, because a landing on water can only ever be a crash. River in her mouth and crashed river in her lungs and down her face or just the crying again, because of course Oksana will leave and forever, and letters will come in her writing or will not, and next to her the almost daughter is exactly who she is, and not almost – and because the water is crushed crystal light around them and because it has to be worth it because they have tried, and later, after she has cried more split river, she will weave and keep winding her *wide shroud of words*, and Oksana's hurtled body next to hers and so much river—

You said we would swim, she says from her lungs when they meet the other naked mouth in the crash. You promised, she says. You promised. I promised.

So this is the last of her own portraits, just for now. Weave it and thread it and hear it and these are her faces, in beads and words and layer-lines, and rush. Remember her. Remember truth. This is her palace. These are her portraits.

Portrait #77
But here, where

... Темный, прямой и взыскательный взгляд.
Взгляд, к обороне готовый.
Юные женщины так не глядят ...
Marina Tsvetaeva, 'Grandmother'

   ... Хотелось бы всех поименно назвать,
    Да отняли список, и негде узнать.
   Для них соткала я широкий покров
  Из бедных, у них же подслушанных слов.
    О них вспоминаю всегда и везде,
     О них не забуду и в новой беде,
   И если зажмут мой измученный рот,
  Которым кричит стомильонный народ,
    Пусть так же они поминают меня
     В канун моего погребального дня.
    А если когда-нибудь в этой стране
  Воздвигнуть задумают памятник мне ...
   Anna Akhmatova, 'Requiem (Epilogue)'

... Не сдавшиеся злобе дня
Глаза, оставшиеся – да! –
Зерцалами самих себя ...
... Девический дагерротип
Души моей ...
Marina Tsvetaeva, 'House'

Acknowledgements

I am grateful to many people for many, many things, but specifically for the existence of this book I would like to thank: Ludo Cinelli, Eve White, Steven Evans, Abigail Scruby, Spread The Word's London Writers Awards, Bobby Nayyar, Aliya Gulamani, Ruth Harrison, Adam Zmith, S. Niroshini, Natasha Brown, Salma Ibrahim, Taranjit Mander, Natalia Ю., Ivan Vasilyev, Memorial Perm and Brigette Manion. To all of you, thank you, thank you, thank you.

This book is a work of fiction but the consequences of silencing are very real.

ORIGINALS

NEW WRITING FROM
BRITAIN'S OLDEST PUBLISHER

2023

She That Lay Silent-Like Upon Our Shore | **Brendan Casey**
A 'wild, wanton, fresh' (*Irish Independent*) fable about human-
ity's relationship with the natural world, crisis and religion.

Stronger than Death | **Francesca Bratton**
A 'profound, moving and courageous' (*Irish Times*) part-
memoir, part-biography of modernist poet Hart Crane's final
year in Mexico.

2022

Catchlights | **Niamh Prior**
A 'clever, literary and intriguing' (*Irish Examiner*) novel in
stories about shallow and deep acts of cruelty, love, selfishness
and kindness which reverberate for years.

Nobody Gets Out Alive | **Leigh Newman**
An exhilarating, 'irresistible' (Jonathan Lee) story collection
about women navigating the wilds of male-dominated
Alaskan society.

Free to Go | **Esa Aldegheri**
One woman's around-the-world adventure, and an 'honest
and perceptive' (Lois Pryce) exploration of borders, freedom
and motherhood.

2021
Penny Baps | **Kevin Doherty**
A beautifully-told debut about the relationship between brothers and the difference between good and bad by a 'new, original voice' (*Irish Times*).

A Length of Road | **Robert Hamberger**
A memoir about love and loss, fatherhood and masculinity, and John Clare, by a Polari Prize-shortlisted poet, 'whose work is rooted in people and relationships' (Jackie Wills).

We Could Not See the Stars | **Elizabeth Wong**
Han must leave his village and venture to a group of islands to discover the truth about his mother–'There is really no book quite like it' (*A Naga of the Nusantara*).

2020
Toto Among the Murderers | **Sally J Morgan**
An 'exhilarating' (Susan Barker) debut novel set in 1970s Leeds and Sheffield when attacks on women punctuated the news.

Self-Portrait in Black and White | **Thomas Chatterton Williams**
An 'extraordinarily thought-provoking' (*Sunday Times*) interrogation of race and identity from one of America's most brilliant cultural critics.

2019
Asghar and Zahra | **Sameer Rahim**
A 'funny, wise and beautifully written' (Colm Tóibín, *New Statesman*) account of a doomed marriage.

Nobber | Oisín Fagan

A wildly inventive and audacious fourteenth-century Irish Plague novel that is 'vigorously, writhingly itself' (*Observer*, Books of the Year).

2018

A Kind of Freedom | Margaret Wilkerson Sexton

A fascinating exploration of the long-lasting and enduring divisive legacy of slavery by a writer of 'uncommon nerve and talent' (*New York Times*).

Jott | Sam Thompson

A 'complex, nuanced novel of extraordinary perception' (*Herald*) about friendship, madness and modernism.

Game Theory | Thomas Jones

A 'well observed and ruthlessly truthful' (*Daily Mail*) comedy about friendship, sex and parenting, and about the games people play.

2017

Elmet | Fiona Mozley

'A quiet explosion of a book, exquisite and unforgettable' (*The Economist*), about a family living on land that isn't theirs.

2016

Blind Water Pass | Anna Metcalfe

A debut collection of stories about communication and miscommunication, between characters and across cultures that 'demonstrates a grasp of storytelling beyond the expectations of any debut author' (*Observer*).

The Bed Moved | Rebecca Schiff
Frank and irreverent, these stories offer a singular view of growing up (or not) and finding love (or not) from 'a fresh voice well worth listening to' (*Atlantic*).

Marlow's Landing | Toby Vieira
An 'economical, accomplished and assured' (*The Times*) novel of diamonds, deceit and a trip up-river.

2015
An Account of the Decline of the Great Auk, According to One Who Saw It | Jessie Greengrass
The twelve stories in this 'spectacularly accomplished' (*The Economist*) collection range over centuries and across the world.

Generation | Paula McGrath
'A hugely ambitious and compelling' (*Irish Times*) novel spanning generations and continents on an epic scale.